Old Goat

Donatien Moisdon

Old Goat   Donatien Moisdon

Thank you

Kelly Dickey
Arkadelphia, Arkansas
for permission to publish the
cover photo

Old Goat   Donatien Moisdon

Table of Contents
Chapter One 4
Chapter Two 13
Chapter Three 16
Chapter Four 19
Chapter Five 26
Chapter Six 39
Chapter Seven 57
Chapter Eight 67
Chapter Nine 81
Chapter Ten 85
Chapter Eleven 117
Chapter Twelve 144
Chapter Thirteen 159
Chapter Fourteen 163
Chapter Fifteen 171
Chapter Sixteen 176
Chapter Seventeen 192
Chapter Eighteen 199
Chapter Nineteen 213
Epilogue 226

Chapter One

1992

Astrologers are always telling gullible females that they will meet a "tall, dark stranger." Peter Lambert was tall and blond. He had the impressive handsome face of a Roman emperor with curly hair and a neatly trimmed beard. Add to this a muscular body, without a trace of fat, and the young man presented you with a pretty good example of male perfection. Unfortunately, he was aware of it and would easily let a superior little smile play on his lips. Like so many good-lookers, he had a split personality: in public, he typically overcompensated for a mediocre mind by means of sterile aggressiveness whereas he became more approachable, almost shy when you were alone with him.

Peter was both impatient and frustrated. After his "A"-Levels, which he only managed to pass by spending two years in the Upper-Sixth, he had wanted to become an RAF pilot but failed to convince the Recruiting Officer that he had what it takes for the job.

Same story when he approached the Fleet Air Arm. If he could not be a pilot, he thought, he would at least become an Army officer. He tried Sandhurst. They laughed him out of town. In desperation, he turned to Customs and entered a training programme but left as soon as he could because, according to him, promotion prospects were not good enough. The truth of the matter was that he had been kicked out. I don't suppose he ever realized to what extent his *Mister Know-it-all* attitude had worked against him. Instructors have little patience with cocky youngsters. Peter ended up working for his father.

I've had many opportunities to get to know Peter's parents and, with hindsight, it helped me understand a lot of things. They were obsessed with money, down to the last penny. At odds with their suppliers, regularly breaking their promises, they were always, by hook or by crook, trying to pull every square inch of the blanket to their side of the bed. Worse still: they loved setting people against one another, a habit that often backfired; but, for them, it was like a drug. They had no intention of giving it up. Planting seeds of hatred in others held the same fascination as, in primitive societies, organizing cock fights. They were not afraid of spreading the most outrageous calumnies; so much so that it had become part of their everyday conversation.

A strong and wiry little man, Andrew Lambert, with his bushy beard, looked very much like a cross between Popeye and one of those missionaries we used to send to Africa. While thinking of himself as being vastly more intelligent than ninety-nine percent of the human race, he could tell lies with such confidence that, at first, most people fell for his gift of the gab and were quite taken in. He did so as if lying was the most natural thing in the world... and for him, it certainly was - to the extent that he must have wondered why anyone would ever bother telling the truth. He despised those who trusted him and hated those who, after a while, stopped doing so. He started an impressive number of sentences with "Personally, I..." or "As far as I am concerned, I..."

Old Goat

Donatien Moisdon

Even when you knew him well, you still caught yourself believing (for a time) in the poisonous fibs he distilled constantly. The mixture of true and false statements in his conversation was so intricate that you never knew where you stood. I came to the conclusion that if he was so convincing, it stemmed from the fact that he probably had no trouble convincing himself in the first place. His grasp of reality was wavy and hazy in an evil sort of way. I would not be surprised to hear that he had ended up in jail or in a mental institution.

...yet he was so clever! His mind was sharp and reacted quickly. Having perfected the art of side-tracking the conversation, all the better to counterattack, he would often turn a situation upside down and, from being the accused, become the accuser. Peter had inherited from his father the certainty that he was always right, but he lacked the wit and charm of the authentic con man.

Andrew Lambert had started life as a shopkeeper. Inevitably, supermarkets and extortionate council taxes had soon threatened his livelihood. He then decided, without undergoing any training or asking anyone's advice (he knew it all, of course) to become a landscape gardener. What he knew, he learnt as he went, never conscious of how much he still had to master. He employed his son, the very same young man who thought he had it in himself to become a pilot or, at the very least, an officer.

In order to set the record straight, I must say that our father-son duo was not exactly work-shy. I often saw them laboring more than ten hours a day in terrible weather conditions: cold, rain, wind... or all three combined. I admired their tenacity, their will to survive and, financially speaking, to keep their heads above water. Back at the house, Andrew had his dinner around eight, then settled down in front of the telly where he fell asleep almost immediately.

More resilient, Peter, after his shower, would, twice a week, drive over to my mother's apartment in his van, and pick me up. We then went to a large caravan, which the Lamberts had equipped as a mobile office. There was a folding bed with a rather thin mattress and rather creaky springs. The place smelt of stationery, Wellington boots, stale tobacco and stale coffee. I was a virgin the first time I went in. Peter was very patient.

Delighted to have attracted the attention of a good-looking man, I wished for nothing more. Marriage was never mentioned between us. What I did find frustrating, however, was the fact that my vagina was always so dry! As it is also very narrow, we invariably had to use Vaseline... all the more intriguing for me, since I had always been oozing with lubrication when playing with myself.

Peter had a hobby which he practiced with an enthusiasm bordering on obsession: electronic surveillance. Instead of trying so desperately to join various branches of the Armed Forces, he should have trained as a spy or a private detective. Just as some people spend a small fortune collecting toy soldiers or building miniature railways,

Peter "invested" – and I found it hard to see what kind of return he got from this "investment" – in all sorts of listening and recording devices. At his Sixth-Form College, he had bugged the office of the headmaster and the teachers' common room. By his own admission, he had never stumbled upon any shattering professional or personal secret. The frisson he experienced came much more from being able to eavesdrop than from the conversations he actually listened to. He had also purchased a special directional, long-range microphone looking like a furry gun. Late at night, he would lower the window of his car and invade the privacy of a house or a flat. He recorded all this and made me listen to long and boring audiotapes. I was subjected to the tantrum of a young woman whose dog had defecated on the doormat, the grumbling of a man who wondered how he was going to pay for urgent repairs on the roof of his property, and the laconic instructions of an invalid woman to her home-help visitor. I honestly did not know how to react to all this. Peter was so vain that my laughter or criticism would have backfired. I used to show a polite amount of interest while never displaying too much enthusiasm. Feeling that I was impressed by his skill was enough to keep him happy. The fact that his spying activities were illegal never seems to have crossed his mind.

There was one thing, however, which I found truly amusing. Spurred on by my reaction, he started doing it a lot: I am talking about tampering with tapes until you heard people make the most absurd statements. A few words or even, at times, just a few syllables cleverly selected, then omitted or re-recorded in another context would turn: "It's been pissing with rain for three days now and with my car out of order, I still have to take that bloody bus every morning." into: "I've been pissing in the bloody bus for three days now." To my surprise, Mother would roar with laughter when Peter played these tapes to her. The example I'm giving is very elementary. Peter could alter entire conversations. He would record verbose politicians and breathless sportsmen from the telly or angry housewives from phone-in radio programmes and make them utter the most outrageous nonsense.

Chapter Two

Ten years with the same boyfriend and twenty years in the same job; twenty years of accepting life as it is without asking too many questions. Whenever I felt a bit low, I would count my blessings. I was working when others were unemployed; I had a regular four-week holiday and a pension plan. Above all, I had "someone," as they say. The fact that the "someone" in question did not want to marry me left me indifferent, mostly because I didn't feel like marrying him either. If you were a meek little mouse wallowing in the worship of your lord and master, then life with Peter could be bearable but I did not fit the bill.

Most of my workmates were married but very few enjoyed a happy life. This observation helped me accept my fate. Single *girls* look for someone with an obsession bordering on hysteria. At thirty-two, Rhonda was all the more desolate that she was in love with a twenty-six-year-old postman who had not the slightest intention of ever tying the knot. She gave him up in order to devote all her time and energy to finding a suitable husband. What she did find was the recipe for a nervous breakdown. Claudia, brought up in a religious family, and still a virgin at twenty-five, was scared of her own shadow. Anita liked to sleep around but could never bring herself to trust a man. After a few dates, she would break up with him on the most futile of reasons. Only Alice and Rosalind, who shared a flat and had sought an escape from the world through their lesbian relationship, seemed to have reached some form of inner calm. I was surrounded by what psychiatrists would have called *cases*, but all these *cases* represent the norm in the end, don't they? Who, among us, can claim never to have been traumatized by poverty, illness, violence, the death of a loved one or the burden of weird parents? These young women were, on the whole, extremely likable, and often harder on themselves than they should have been.

They were envious of the stable, argument-free relationship between Peter and me. They could not see, of course, to what extent that relationship was void of sentimental, erotic and poetic dimension.

At what time in our lives do we decide no longer to wait for such a dimension in love? Have we ever expected any? To be seen in town with a handsome male, occasionally to watch TV with him, and to be screwed twice a week in the missionary position was what most women eventually accept as the definition of happiness. For everything else, there is always Mills & Boon.

At thirty-eight I was not very different from what I looked like ten or even twenty years before. Plain features make a teenager look older. However, as years go by, the face hardly changes and people start saying: "She's not bad looking for her age;" and it is true that I had never felt less… ordinary. I almost said *ugly* but that would be wrong. With every decade I become more and more convinced that I have never been ugly. Maybe it was all in my mind. With more self-confidence, I might have decided that I was good-looking.

Chapter Three

I clearly remember **his** first visit. I was standing on a table, wearing only the bottom half of a lime-green bikini. It was just a little too loose around the buttocks and had to be adjusted. The girls would come close to me, then walk away, then come back... They would pinch the material and shake it gently between thumb and index. They inserted their fingers under the elastics and pulled them this way or that way. It tickled a bit. Various suggestions were made.

As usual, Cyril, leaning against the doorframe of his office, surveyed the situation without saying much. He was a tall, lean, redhead individual with thinning hair and blotchy complexion. He was also a one-man show: owner, manager, supervisor, accountant and secretary of his firm which he had simply called "Cyril's." One hand under his chin, his eyes narrowed into slits like those of a hunter spotting prey in the desert, he was (bless him) quite blind to the slim, practically naked body parading in front of him. He stared only at the garment... or so I thought at the time.

Next to Cyril, that day, stood a fat little man in his early sixties. His balding head, with slightly bulging eyes, was cocked to one side. His thick lips moved as he whispered something to Cyril. He wore an impeccable mouse-coloured three-piece suit. His shiny brown shoes reflected the spotlights from the sewing machines. When he moved, we realized that one of his legs was shorter than the other and that he used a walking stick. All the same, he exuded an impressive stage presence, and we were somewhat intimidated. During the next few days, he came back several times.

"Cyril, who's that?" asked the girls.

"A big buyer... potentially."

"He sure is big, anyway."

"Ha, ha!"

His name was Lawrence Drover; Mister Drover for us. Cyril never mentioned his first name.

Chapter Four

I like gardening. Actually, no: I don't really like gardening because I don't know anything about it, but I like working in a garden, so long as someone else tells me what to do. I am in awe of people who can slide their palms under the leaves of a plant and whisper lovingly something like: "Ah, yes." (there follows a mile-long Latin double name) "It needs shade and not too much water. It thrives in light soil with very little chalk. If you clip it properly in the Autumn, it will give you loads of gorgeous flowers the year after." How can they remember all that? On the other hand, they are probably the same people who would not be able to tell the difference between cretonne, poplin and organdie.

Lawrence Drover did like gardening. For him, it was more than a hobby: it was an overwhelming commitment. The first time I saw him at close range was on a late afternoon, on a Tuesday. He had pulled outside of my mother's flat in his gray Citroën and walked up to our front door. I let him in. He was dressed in something that he must have bought in an Army surplus store: boots with prominent metal eyelets, khaki trousers with camouflage patterns, heavy dark-green sweater with leather patches. He smelled... not bad, but fairly strong. I could detect a faint mixture of compost and horse manure. Mum had watched him come out of the car and, just like my workmates, had exclaimed: "Who's that?" She had then added: "He looks like an old goat."

"He's one of Cyril's customers."

"But what's he doing here?"

"No idea."

He apologized for the way he was dressed and for the fact that he had shown up without warning. He accepted a cup of tea. Not for a second did my mother and I suspect that his presence had anything to do with some sort of attraction he could have felt for me.

Old Goat

Donatien Moisdon

"May I borrow your daughter tomorrow evening?" he asked in a deep, husky voice while dropping a lump of sugar in his tea. At first, I thought he had a cold in the chest, but it turned out to be his normal voice. He may have looked like an old goat to my mother but, to me, he was more like an old tortoise. Asking Mum if *I* could go out was a bit much... almost insulting, in fact. I hardly looked like a kid. I was the one who answered: "What do you want to borrow me for?"

"I'd like your opinion on a project I have been tossing around in my head: cream-coloured, turtle-neck sweaters with the name of a university on the chest or along the sleeves."

"Which university?"

"Any at all, my dear Jane: Cambridge, London, Bristol. It doesn't matter. The garment remains the same. Only the print varies."

"Like a T-shirt?"

"Same principle, only this one will be very good quality. Something that students who have a little money can go for... something which would not look wrong on a professor."

I wondered what sort of preconceived ideas he had regarding professors. I could see them, sometimes, coming out of our local university, dressed like vagrants, especially those from the Sociology Department. Most of the others seemed to be wearing the same old tweed jackets with pregnant pockets and shapeless dark trousers day after day, not that these gentlemen were poor in any way, especially when comparing their incomes to those of a seamstress; but they appeared to enjoy this phony proletarian look. Women professors, on the other hand, were harder to identify at first. Yet, after a while, you got to spot their mock designer suits, their stiff gaits, their chins stuck in the air and the look on their faces which seem to say: "I have a PhD and I am a very busy, very important person, so get out of my way, peasant, and drop dead."

Drover went on: "I could well see it within the £250 to £300 range... retail."

"But why ask me? You should talk to Cyril."

"I will talk to Cyril when it comes to manufacturing costs. I am talking to you because you have good taste."

Considering that, with the exception of the time when he had seen me wearing only half a bikini, I had always been hiding from head to foot under a white smock, I did not understand how he could think of me as a person of good taste. He must have read the doubts on my face because he added: "I've passed you in the street a few times. Once, you were at a book fair with a couple of young men. I've also seen you window-shopping all by yourself. From the start, I was struck by your elegance. Even today, at home, you look remarkable."

I was wearing a very finely knitted, long-sleeved, dark-brown sweater over matching corduroy trousers. All I could answer was: "But I didn't see you."

"I obviously didn't make much of an impression."

He smiled. It was the first time I saw him smile, really smile and showing his bright, healthy, front teeth. It changed him completely, and I caught sight of my mother's eyes widening under the shock. Drover was suddenly becoming young and charming. The old goat had turned into a natural, approachable seducer.

"Oh, no, it's not that at all." I stammered while Mum rushed over to pour another cup of tea and almost spilled some in the process. *Heck,* I thought, *she's falling for him.* Within the next split second, I pictured myself with Drover as my stepfather and that made me burst out laughing.

"You have a lovely laugh," he said, before taking a sip from his cup.

"I wasn't laughing at you, honest."

"Do you know who said that money is the greatest aphrodisiac?"

"No."

"Sam Goldwin."

"Don't know him."

He smiled again. "I disagree with him, actually. I would say that laughter is the greatest aphrodisiac."

I told him I would let myself be borrowed for an evening.

"I'll pick you up tomorrow night, then," he said as he got up.

"Oh, please don't. I'll ask my boyfriend to give me a lift."

There were a few seconds of embarrassment then he added: "Very well.... but I'll bring you back here."

"Fine."

I wanted to share with Peter this exciting episode in my otherwise rather dull and gray life, his own life being hardly more fascinating than mine.

Chapter Five

"The old geezer's got the hots for you," announced Peter as we headed for Drover's house. The white van smelled of earth and power tools. I had spread a blanket on the passenger seat, as I didn't trust its apparent cleanliness.

"Of course not. He could be my father."

"It's got nothing to do with it. Hey, listen to that."

He pushed a cassette in the dashboard player and I was treated to a conversation between a man and a woman on genealogy. It seemed that the woman was quite an expert in the field. The man was asking her if she could help him locate one of his ancestors, called Jane, like me, who might have emigrated to the States in the 1830s or 40s.

"Super, don't you think?" asked Peter.

"Super. Tell me: have you ever recorded people making love?"

"Yeah, my parents."

"You're a pig." But I said it laughing because any serious criticism would have made him fly into a rage. Fortunately, he too laughed (or rather sniggered). We had reached our destination.

"So, here we are," he said. "Didn't he tell you that we should park by the beach and walk the rest of the way?"

"Yes. You can't park on the street. Double yellow lines and all that, and he doesn't want to have to open the gates just to let you turn around. Must be another hundred yards or so."

The car park overlooked the seashore. During the day, vehicles would line up at the edge, facing the ocean. Even in bad weather people would come here, stay in their cars for indeterminate lengths of time and gaze dreamily at the waves and the lashing rain. Tonight, the place was deserted and not a little sinister. We left the van after noisily slamming the sliding doors. Gusts of salty, humid wind enveloped us. We were in one of those little towns, which are like an extended suburb of a mother-town, but still with some countryside all around. How long would this provincial feeling last?

Mr. Drover had mentioned 8 p.m. and it was pitch dark. The streets, which were poorly lit and totally deserted, gave the impression of being both safe and menacing. While Peter and I walked towards the address, our steps echoed as loud as if we had been tapping on frozen ground. Above us, in the blackness of the sky, invisible heads of tall cypress trees moaned and creaked like evil spirits. Occasionally, a howling gust of wind would cover the deep, sucking sounds of close-by waves rolling beach pebbles back and forth.

"I feel like a pimp taking one of his girls to a dirty old man" whispered Peter.

"Jealous?"

"Just joking. Mind you, you do look very elegant tonight."

"You are jealous Peter, because I am always very elegant, but it's the first time you noticed."

"But you smell so good!"

I just gave him a filthy look. Under my black winter coat, I was wearing a white shirt – a man's shirt in fact – with lovely cuff links that had been given to me by a rep. They were oval-shaped. On a gold-speckled background, you could see the five rings of the Olympic Games with, underneath, the letters USA. For "the South," as Cyril used to say, rust-coloured cord trousers. Before leaving the house, I had showered, dabbed my most expensive perfume on my neck, and slipped on a pair of silver-white panties with a triangular lace motif at the front. When you are too poor to afford a car or a holiday in the Bahamas, you indulge in £45 underwear.

On second thought, Peter may not have been wrong to feel a little jealous. I had acted exactly as if I was getting ready for an important date, and he must have sensed it. I wanted to be perfect, down to the smallest, intimate detail. If anyone had suggested that I wanted to have sex with the old Goat, I would have burst out laughing. So? Why go through all this trouble? Why do we do the things we do?

We had reached the correct street number. Peter whistled: "What a pad! It's not a house, it's a mansion."

"Course not: just a large house."

At the end of a graveled courtyard surrounded by walls with, on the street side, black cast-iron railings, stood Drover's house. It was lit by spotlights, probably for our benefit. It obviously dated back to the 1880s and was typical of what they built for small-town VIPs in those days: doctors, chemists, solicitors… The front door was reached by a couple of stone steps and, on either side of that door, on the ground floor, were two tall windows with very small glass panes; there were five more windows in the same style on the upper floor. Under the eaves of the slate roof, an ornate overhang softened the rigidity of this rectangular building. On the left, a Virginia creeper snaked onto the gray-white expanse of the walls. A wisteria hugged the right-hand corner. Dark green masses of various bushes lined the courtyard walls.

I pressed the bell. I could not hear if it rang but it did trigger some heavy barking. Behind one of the downstairs windows, I could see two huge heads jumping up and down, trying to catch sight of the intruder. The main door opened, and Drover shouted: "Come on in." I turned the handle of a small door set into the iron gate. It had not been locked. Peter tried to follow me but I pushed him back firmly: "What are you thinking? Are you crazy?"

Leaning on his walking stick, Drover was waiting for me on top of the steps. The dogs had stopped barking and were trying to insert their heads between his legs. When I had closed the metal door, and he could actually hear the "click" in the lock, Drover let the dogs go. They rushed towards me. The bigger and more impressive of the two, a Beauceron, stopped only a few inches from my shins then turned round and ran back to his master, then back to me. He did this several times. The other one, a black Labrador, kept jumping around me until his head was level with mine.

"Don't let him get you all muddy," said Drover. "He could have dirty paws. Also, I forgot to warn you about dog stools: I remove them twice a day, but you never know."

"What are their names?"

"Pyrrhus for the Labrador and Xenophon for the other one. Zeno for short. Pyrrhus is very affectionate: a little too much at times. Zeno is more distant. He is not the one that will jump all over you and ruin your clothes."

For me, it turned out to be the opposite, at least as far as affection was concerned. I liked Pyrrhus but he often became too insistent. I had to push him back. He would then go and sulk on his carpet and sigh deeply to make me feel guilty, whereas Zeno loved me in a more... adult fashion. I know it's silly, but I could see something human in the eyes of that dog. I was inordinately fond of him.

"He loves you" Drover would say dreamily, as Zeno rested his chin on the tip of my shoe whenever I sat down.

Very formally, the big man had offered to take my coat as I came in. He had also praised the way I was dressed as he wobbled over to a downstairs bedroom to leave the coat on a bed. He then led me to a white, open-worked, metallic table of a style used on garden lawns and patios in Edwardian times. On it was a tray with a beautiful silver teapot and two Coalport cups with matching sugar bowl and milk jug.

"Tea here or in front of the fireplace?" he asked.

I had, during my childhood and adolescence, been envious of, and amazed by, the comfort of houses and flats I had visited, but on that day, I was completely overwhelmed by the elegance I saw around me. It was a discrete form of elegance because, after all, through cinema and television, we all know what "rich" houses look like, just as we know what Saint Mark's Cathedral looks like in Venice, even if we've never been there. There was no trace of extravagance between these walls; they simply made you feel so good! On top of the warmth and comfort that I often found at other people's, this house mothered you without choking you.

Deep couches, huge hi-fi stacks and gleaming kitchens had always made me feel as if the owners had, in turn, been taken over by their possessions and had become their slaves. I went "Wow, Ooooh!" and "Aaaaah!" but couldn't fail experiencing a slight feeling of oppression. No such emotion at Drover's. I felt so free and light that I wanted to dance. A very subtle smell of woodfire was mixed with those of his latest meal: fish in *beurre blanc* I would've said. I had walked into an enchanted world and, as the apostles said during the transfiguration: "Let us remain here." I never wanted to leave the soporific beauty of the place.

I plumbed for the hearth where a log fire was crackling away. We were in an immense living room (immense for me) surrounded on two sides by bookshelves from floor to ceiling. I looked at the books avidly. Even from a distance, I could spot *Remembrance of Things past*, art albums, row upon row of leather-bound collections, biographies of famous composers... The fire was alive, spitting, whispering, turning red or yellow. My cheeks were pleasantly burning. The dogs, flopping out on the Persian carpet, gave such a solid impression of domestic permanence and felicity that I remained silent for a very long time, slowly recovering from this unexpected cultural and environmental impact. My silence did not seem to bother Drover in the least. He too seemed to enjoy the meditative quality of the moment.

Old Goat   Donatien Moisdon

After tea, we went back to the iron table and, on it, Drover showed me patterns, swatches and rough drawings he had fetched from upstairs. I noticed that when he went up, the dogs trotted along to the first step but no further. The bedrooms were out of bounds for them, and they knew it.

By contrast with some of my former school friends and workmates, I have no problem expressing myself or enunciating properly. I don't see the point of torturing or despising a language. I hate to see signs such as "This door is alarmed." Nor do I attempt to speak "posh." I'm happy with just proper, neutral English; I simply avoid lapsing into an estuary accent. Drover noticed it and complimented me. This seemed to create a sort of subtle conspiracy between us.

I was much more hesitant when came the time to give my opinion on the articles of clothing he had mentioned; at least to start with, because without ever going too far or interrupting him, I was slowly gaining in confidence. I was also gaining his trust. From my few years of Latin, I had retained the story of the cobbler who must confine himself to judging shoes and not presume that he can go higher. "*Sutor, ne supra crepidam*" I quoted when Drover tried to push me too far. He looked at me dreamily, said nothing, but smiled and shook his head as if to mean, "*I don't believe this.*"

"Next time, you will have dinner with me." he announced at the end of the evening while he was helping with my coat. It was said softly and politely but also with a quiet touch of firmness. He did not expect a rebuff and did not get one. We went out into the front yard, gravel croaking under our feet. Drover opened the gates while I headed for his car. Through the windowpanes, the dogs were watching us with a hurt and reproachful expression on their faces.

"So? How was it?" Peter asked eagerly when he saw me again the next day. I snapped: "You mean, you didn't record our wild lovemaking?" He gave me a dirty look but, for the first time ever, I saw him blush rather. We were in his father's caravan, and he was undressing quickly. I was doing the same but much more slowly. He no longer looked at me avidly when I was naked. To be fair, I had also lost all interest and fascination for his physical appearance. After ten years, we had become an old couple and fallen into a routine. We had stopped kissing ages ago. As soon as we got into bed, he would simply embrace me, stroke my nape gently for a few seconds then push me on my back, lubricate me with a dab of Vaseline and, in the never-changing missionary position, penetrate me and start his back-and-forth movements. In a few seconds, it was all over. I no longer had orgasms, but it didn't seem to bother him at all.

Chapter Six

My first "dinner" with Drover was rather odd: a revelation of simplicity and good humor. A cleaning woman came every day except Saturdays and Sundays, but he liked to cook for himself. On that particular evening, he appeared in a bright red apron with, printed on it, white frilly panties and bra.

He approached the stove with the determination of a duelist. He had previously prepared some buckwheat pancake batter and grilled chipolatas. Eyes shining with excitement, a big smile stuck on his face, he obviously experienced so much pleasure in cooking his pancakes, then rolling them around a reheated sausage, that he looked to me like a kid absorbed in a fantasy game where he was both a monarch and one of his subjects. He challenged me to make a pancake, and I did quite well despite the enormous weight of the cast-iron pan. The sausages were wonderful. They did not contain a trace of the rubbish one would normally find in factory-made bangers, only minced pork, herbs and spices. He told me later that he regularly got them from an Italian butcher.

We ate while standing in the kitchen, one hand holding the pancake, the other one, palm up, trying not to let drops of fat fall on the floor or over our clothes. Laughing like airhead girls, we wiped our chins with kitchen towels. It was on that occasion that he asked me to stop calling him Mr. Drover and simply use Lawrence. I was relieved: the Mr. Drover ceremonial was beginning to bother me. Peter was furious when I told him.

Wednesday followed Wednesday; month followed month. "The old geezer has got the hots for you," Peter kept saying.

"Course not. Besides, he hates women."

"Is he a queer fellow?"

"Don't be silly. He is divorced. His wife was a cold-hearted creature, a selfish bitch who criticized and humiliated him constantly."

"I see. It's the usual pattern: *My wife doesn't understand me.* Can't you see that all his whining is just meant to soften the potential mistress?"

"So, you double as a shrink now?

But I suspected that, somehow, he had listened in. Lawrence had talked at great length about his marriage. He came from a titled family and was, really, born in a castle, but since his parents had had something like eight children, the estate had to be sold. Dreamily, he would recall the big hall lining the whole length of the building, where he and his brothers and sisters used to slide on foot cushions like skaters on a frozen lake. He laughed as he described the home-made swing hanging from an enormous oak tree in the park. He would invite girls from the village and let them go on the swing in the hope of catching sight of their panties. He still hankered for the wooden cabin built in amongst the branches of another oak tree. He mentioned the horses, one of which was responsible for his crooked leg, just after he had returned from his National Service. "Now, why couldn't that riding accident have happened before?" he added. "I would not have been called up."

And no, he did not want to go back to that place. . .ever, ever. It had been purchased by an honest-to-God family and had not lost its soul by being turned into a hotel, a golf club or a so-called rehabilitation center for young criminals.

Once, and for no apparent reason, he showed me a painted miniature dating back to the eighteenth century where, in front of a rectangular château, not very big, not very impressive, but oozing good taste and charm, stood a middle-aged couple clad as they used to at the time, in hats, ribbons, lace, satin breeches for the man, long dress for the woman. . . an Irish setter walked in front of them. "This, my dear Jane," Lawrence had said in a voice suddenly free from its usual coarseness and now almost velvety, "This is Heyleck Hall."

I am still cross with myself for not catching on immediately. With a half-numbed mind, I asked: "Heyleck Hall? What's that?"

"That is where I was born and grew up. Maybe you'll understand better now why this house, which seems so big to you, gives me the feeling of living in a rabbit hutch. . . a very pretty rabbit hutch. Don't misunderstand . . . I love it. When I bought it, it had been neglected for so long that it was completely covered with vegetation, not unlike a Cambodian temple lost in the jungle. You could barely see it from the street. All the wooden frames were rotten, and the roof threatened to collapse, but I fell for it immediately. It's like being in love, you know, we never quite understand why. . ."

*

This was a period of my life when I may have been drinking too much. I never got drunk but often finished the evening floating on air in a rather delightful way, only to end up wrestling during the night, with obsessive, claustrophobic, sweaty dreams. Before each of our regular Wednesday evening meals, Lawrence and I had aperitifs.

When, for the first time, he opened the mahogany bar, as long as a pirogue, and asked what my favorite poison was, my lower jaw had dropped: outside of pubs, I had never seen such an assortment of bottles. I let him choose for me. He suggested that I should try his usual mix: a cream sherry poured over a squirt of gin. On a couple of small plates, he had laid out slivers of Cheddar, Emmental, Comté and Tomme Brûlée.

Lawrence made me appreciate wines. It was a revelation. At the start of our first real meal, that is to say a sitting-down dinner and not just pancakes gobbled up in the middle of the kitchen, he had casually poured a bottle of 15-year-old Châteauneuf-du-Pape into a decanter. Seeing how I reacted after the first few sips, he promised to make me try many other kinds. I had never dreamt that wine could taste so good. I then suspected that 99% of the population probably doesn't either. The price, for one thing, is a bit daunting. The very next day,

I sneaked into a rather exclusive-looking wine shop and asked for a similar wine. "£96 a bottle Madam," the smarmy salesman replied.

"I just love a guest who can appreciate the best things in life," Lawrence whispered. "I'll turn you into an expert." I was a willing student, my best excuse being that I did not have a car and therefore did not have to drive home. Eager to share the delights of good wines with me, Lawrence, who, for the first few weeks, had only had one glass during the meal, decided that, from then on, I would take a taxi. No, that WE would take a taxi. He would bring me back to my mother's and return to his place alone.

After the meal – during which the bottle of wine ended its career – Lawrence offered a *digestif*. I tried several liqueurs, each more delicious than the one before and, after a while, regularly asked for Drambuie. To this day, if given some, I find it very hard not to burst into tears.

"How did you manage to marry a woman who didn't love you?" I asked one evening.

By then, we had reached the stage when neither of us carried on with the pretense that I had come to discuss potential articles of clothing. Peter no longer drove me, Lawrence would send a taxi. We had a well-honed Wednesday routine. It was a marvelous mid-week form of entertainment and relaxation. Lawrence did the cooking, opened yet another one of his excellent vintage bottles and we would eat slowly, taking all the time in the world to appreciate both food and drink while carrying on some inconsequential conversation; then, followed by the dogs, we would settle in front of the fireplace, Lawrence in his armchair and me in 'mine.' We remained the whole time several feet apart from each other, all very fine and proper - almost Victorian - I'd say. Most of the time, just happy to be together, we spoke little or not at all. With the help from a generous intake of alcohol, I floated on a cloud of happiness and felt completely cut off from the rest of the world.

"How did I come to marry a heartless wife?" Lawrence repeated. "Lack of experience, that's all. I grew up in a nice, charitable, accessible family who were not in the least bit snotty, but very religious. The atmosphere was usually relaxed and cheerful. You were allowed to talk about love but never about sex. The religious brainwashing I have been subjected to was quite thorough, but for some reason, never got hold of me.

One day, my younger brother arrived unexpectedly with a guest: a colleague of his at university; not a girlfriend, just a friend who happened to be a girl. I was overwhelmed - and soon became hypnotized by her intelligence and her brilliance, not to mention her extremely good looks. She was, at the time, writing a PhD thesis in entomology and had already established herself within her circle of specialists with an impressive array of articles on all sorts of creepy crawlies I had never heard of. She had trekked through the Brazilian jungle, climbed inhospitable mountains, shot an anaconda who fancied her for breakfast, slept in leech-and-mosquito-infested swamps, you name it – she was the Indiana Jones of the insect world. She lapped up the fact that I was in awe of her.

We seemed to get along fine and so we got married. Within a few months, however, I was no longer blind and could perceive the true nature of that woman. Fiona was, and still is, a remarkable individual but she is also extremely intolerant of anything that does not fit in exactly with her views. She started humiliating me in public as she clearly believed that any difference in our tastes and habits was proof positive that I had brains the size of a walnut."

We were quite far from the traditional *My wife doesn't understand me* as imagined by Peter's elementary psychology. "So, you got a divorce?" I asked timidly.

"So, we got a divorce. I had rushed into marriage because I was twenty-eight years old, just as one rushes to the beach because it's August and a lovely day. Nothing more."

"And now?"

"Now, I know what love is. I fell in love. I mean, really fell in love for the first time only seven years ago. The woman liked me but did not love me. She would not leave her husband. After that, a much younger woman fell in love with me. I knew it wouldn't last because she was wealthy."

"Even more than you?"

Oops! I bit my lips, but it was too late. The bloomer had come out. Lawrence could not help laughing: "Oh, yes. A lot more. You see, my dear Jane, I make what most people would call *good money* but I'm only middle-class, even if I was born in a castle. Natasha – as this young, beautiful and brainless creature was called – had a yearly income of roughly £850,000 from her stock market investments alone. If you took into account the rents from a string of properties, she was 'worth,' as they say nowadays, close to twelve million Pounds; but even that is nothing."

"Nothing?"

"No. Some of my American clients are worth ten times as much. Yes," he added dreamily "at least ten times as much."

"Is it impossible for a rich woman to find love?"

"It can happen, I suppose, but it's extremely rare. Rich girls are not brought up to give, they are brought up to take. To them, *giving* always means giving money. They think everyone is after their money and that everyone is envious of their wealth. *Giving*, of course, has nothing to do with money. *Giving* means being generous with your time, your smile, your affection, your consideration for others, your interest in others. . . but the rich wouldn't know what you are talking about. All these qualities have been removed from their hearts and they are like mummies, sealed away in a crypt. A rich girl may indeed fall in love with a man, just as a child falls in love with a toy, but there is only one person in the whole world that she can truly love: and that's herself."

"Rather sad. I would like to find love and I am not rich."

"What about that young gorilla you go out with? Don't you love him?"

I laughed all the more easily that there wasn't a trace of contempt in Lawrence's tone of voice. On the contrary, I seemed to detect a certain underlying admiration for those young *gorillas*, capable of delivering a 50 lb. sack of cement as casually as a postman would hand you a letter. "No, I don't love him, and he doesn't love me either."

"Then why...? No, I'm sorry, I have no right to pry."

"I'll tell you just the same. I am with him so that I can say: *I've got someone.* At work, at the workshop, we say: *She's got someone* or: *She's found someone.* We are pleased for those who have found someone and feel sorry for those who haven't. Above all, I guess, we are scared stiff of ever finding ourselves without someone."

"Is it so important?"

I did not answer and lost myself in the contemplation of the burning logs, the outline of which had turned into glowing-red scales. From time to time, a flickering tongue of fierce blue would run from scale to scale, or else a log would collapse with a swishing sound and send up a small firework display of golden sparks.

*

The next day, I left Peter. It was not the best time to do so. An angry customer whom he and his father had defrauded with cheap material and faulty workmanship was suing their small company. I wasn't interested in the details. I would have been if, emotionally speaking, Peter and I had been closer. I kept thinking long and hard about Lawrence's remark. Why indeed, should I live my life in order to conform to what others might or might not think of me?

"What would people think?" My mother used to say when I was little and tried to do something like having my hair cut as short as a boy's. What would people think now if I could not say that *I have someone?* Those who find me likable would still like me. Those who do not like me would add another barb to their collection of nasty remarks, but the vast majority would not give a damn.

They have their own worries...

That night, I let Peter do what he wanted with me, which wasn't much. Very predictably, it was all over in a matter of minutes. I thought he would be less angry if he was sexually satisfied. His frustration, I felt, would grow later. After I got dressed, I kissed him lightly on the forehead. "I am leaving you, Peter. You no longer give me any pleasure. I think I'd like to be by myself from now on." I had, for a fleeting moment, the temptation of adding *I hope we shall remain friends,* but I bit my tongue. All Peter needed was a vagina, not a friend.

He remained gob-smacked, catatonic, trying to say something, but it got stuck in his throat. He finally blurted out: "Wwww...what? **You** are leaving **me**? That's the best one yet! A plain girl like you! You'll never find anyone else, d'you hear me? Never!" I smiled. His vulgar and selfish outburst was something of a relief. It made things easy; much easier than if he had started to cry or asked me to marry him. *No way*, I thought, *will I come down to your level and start a shouting match.* "Never find anyone else?" *That's possible. Who knows? But a good vibrator will be better than you.*

"You laugh." He went on angrily.

At first, I absolutely did not understand what he meant. True, I had smiled very briefly but I certainly had not laughed. I was not even smirking. "You laugh all the time when you are with him, don't you?" He was screaming like a spoiled child who refuses to share a toy. Then, with a pathetic whine, he went on: "You never laughed like that with me."

Laughter is the greatest aphrodisiac; Lawrence had said on the day of his first visit to my mother's. Indeed, Peter and I had not laughed. Peter had sometimes sniggered when mentioning people he despised – and the list was long – but we had never indulged in the delightfully silly laughter that true lovers specialize in. For the first and last time, I felt a little sorry for him.

Our affair had truly been as cold as that frame of aluminum door on which my hand was resting. I took one last look at the Spartan interior of the Portacabin, half-office, half-bedroom, hoping nevertheless to detect the presence of a few good memories but it had never been a love nest, just a sordid cubicle. From this last visit, all I took with me was the sight of depressing surroundings smelling of stale tobacco, the presence of a creaky folding bed and its thin mattress. . . metal chairs, a tubular desk, Peter's clothes strewn on the floor and Peter himself standing rigid and naked, with a hateful rictus on his lips. I shivered, feeling sad. Feeling ashamed also that, for ten years, I had been yielding to a natural yearning for sex. On the other hand, I was glad that I had never taken this relationship too seriously and that I had never fallen in love. I had stayed with Peter all this time because no one else was interested in me, nor was I obsessed with getting married and having children, which might have encouraged me to seek help from a marriage bureau or a computer dating club.

"Goodbye, Peter" I said calmly, as I went out in the cool night air. *Yes, indeed*, I added inwardly, *I need some fresh air in more ways than one.*

Chapter Seven

2002

I live in a council flat nowadays, as befits a person of my condition. The area isn't too bad; there are no graffiti on the walls, neighbors do not make the walls shake with Rap; people can leave their cars on the street of an evening and, in the morning, find that their pride and joy has retained its radio and all four wheels.

I am on the third floor and there is no lift. I don't care. Maybe I will moan about it one day but why should I worry now? I was very lucky to be allocated a two-bedroom flat, a rare thing for a single *girl*. In spite of my modest income, I managed to decorate it tastefully; at least I hope I did. I was not aiming for luxury; I simply tried to give an impression of calm, restful neatness. I was helped by the fact that there are people who throw away some beautiful pieces of furniture. I even found a coffee table made of cherry wood.

Old Goat   Donatien Moisdon

My childhood was spent in the midst of a chaotic, worn out, bric-a-brac. Everything felt as if it was only temporary. First-time visitors thought that we had just moved in, and suggested that, eventually, we would *do something* with the place, a remark that put my mother on edge, and invariably made me laugh. She also bristled when being told, "This apartment has a lot of potential;" but its mediocrity was immutable. Now, in a place of my own, I can partially recreate the feeling I used to have when visiting other people: that of being in normal surroundings with very nice – if modest – furniture.

When I left school, I was at an impasse. I could not go on to university, nor did I have any training likely to secure some sort of employment. Apart from sewing, I couldn't do anything, not even type. Inevitably, I ended up in a sweatshop: low wages, long hours. . . At least I was lucky enough to find one that wasn't crammed with illegal immigrants, and where everything was above board, from mandatory contributions to the possibility of belonging to a Trade Union.

Old Goat   Donatien Moisdon

At the end of a day's work, I did not feel like rushing back to my mother's depressing place. I much preferred accepting all kinds of invitations: movies, a walk on the beach, an aimless drive in someone's car or, at weekends, a stadium seat at a gymnastics competition. I have not really changed; I still hope for a colleague's suggestion of some activity or other. I have never learnt to "live with myself" as they say. I adore my little flat, to which I always repair with great relief and gratitude when I am tired, but as soon as I feel better, I become, once more, worried, insecure, restless. . .

I have a few friends but no lover; I mean, no real lover, i.e. one with whom I would long to be most of the time, one I would rush to, the minute I left work. I see Michael now and then, once or twice a month, perhaps. He is retired. He loves me; he gives me magnificent orgasms, but I am not in love with him. In the course of a typical day, I never think about him. When I start missing the intense pleasure he gives me, I telephone, and he shows up, cheerful, enthusiastic, and as always, eager to treat me to another demonstration of his amazing manual and lingual techniques. No penetration. The poor dear is past it. His presence, however, is hardly indispensable. He is an aging toy boy, and he loves it. There is, within me, something broken: a spring, of course, to use the accepted cliché. I don't think I will ever have what it takes to rekindle passionate love. Like that of a discarded clock, my spring spills out of my soul and hangs, listless and useless.

In addition to my old lover, I know two male homosexual friends with whom I often go out. They were both initiated by their priests when they were respectively chorister and choirboy in two different parishes. Christopher is gaunt and quiet. Daniel, by contrast, is a real poppy and I love him like a little brother. He is in his late twenties, and he adores me. What can he find in the company of a forty-eight-year-old woman? A mother figure? At first, this question bothered me, but no longer. I know that it has never bothered him. After all, why can't a young teacher make friends with a middle-aged school cleaner, which is what I became after I left Cyril's? It is improbable but there is no law against it.

Daniel looks at the world with wide, laughing eyes, as if he saw it for the first time and was incapable of grasping its intrinsic ugliness. The two of us – or the three of us if Christopher tags along – go to art galleries, book fairs or other cultural events within the capabilities of a provincial town.

Last Summer, Daniel spent a night at my place - in my bed, in fact. The second bedroom is so full of all sorts of things that there is no room for anything else, not even a single bed. Still possessed by love for thread, material, needles and sewing machines, I am fortunate to have an area where I can immerse myself in my hobby without turning the whole flat into a mess. Christopher was planning to come over and fetch Daniel but there had been a confusing story of lost car keys, the details of which I do not remember and do not care about. Daniel had cuddled me from behind and, through his underwear and my nightgown, I had been conscious of his erection.

"You want to make love to a woman, now?" I asked.

"No, but it feels so good being here with you!"

I turned over and slipped my hand in his underpants. He did not protest. I started to stroke him slowly then more and more firmly and quickly. He had a long and noisy orgasm. Several weeks after this episode, he would still become as red as a tomato whenever we met, especially if Christopher happened to be around.

When I don't hang out with Daniel and Christopher, I sometimes go for a drive with Yves and Gwen. Gwen is a teacher at the school where I work. You don't get bored with those two. They argue all the time. They have been together for seventeen years. Well, not really *together*. Two or three times, she moved in with him or he moved in with her, but it never worked out and they regularly *divorced* in spectacular and theatrical fashion. Right now, they each have their own flat. The fact that, during the few weeks of cold war following each bitter separation Gwen receives the attentions of a gigantic and extremely good-looking Jamaican does not really help. She now has two adorable coffee-coloured boys.

Lately, Yves got hold of a motor-caravan. Whenever Gwen can leave the children with her own parents, she and Yves go on a camping weekend and, strangely enough, they often invite me along. Maybe they need an umpire to keep them from killing each other but, by Sunday night, I am exhausted. I start the week more tired than I had been on the Friday.

Yves is a spoiled child, self-centered, demanding, but far from stupid. He can also be kind, helpful and generous. He is talented in many ways (as a photographer, for instance) and elegant in his manners and speech. Like Peter, like me, like so many people I know, Yves has failed at everything he tried and must be content with a low-paid job. He drives a florist's delivery van.

Gwen, a small, wiry, hyperactive woman, is known for her aggressively feminist views and a talent for sarcastic remarks. What mysterious attraction can so irrevocably – if intermittently – bring these two incompatible individuals together? It's enough to make you believe in curses.

And then, an hour's drive down the road, in a dusty, sleepy village, live Mark and Jacky. They too invite me over to their house from time to time. I am always welcome. We don't do much: a walk along the seafront or an evening of watching television. Mark and Jacky have not been together for very long. Mark's previous partner was a certain Dorothy, a fascinating woman who had lusted after me. Little by little, flattered by the interest she showed, and also led by what had, by then, become a mixture of curiosity and genuine attraction on my part, I allowed her to make love to me while Mark looked on with undisguised delight. Sometimes he was allowed to join in. Good clean fun, really. When Dorothy left, she went to live with another woman.

Jackie is much more conventional, and Mark has never dared ask her to play exhibition games with me. He never even mentioned our past activities. Jackie is not jealous of my presence. It must be, again, the result of our age difference. She and Mark are in their thirties and, for Jackie, decades are in airtight – or should I say sex-tight – compartments, not unlike mating between different species. Apart from Michael, all my friends are so much younger than me! I wish I knew a psychiatrist and could ask him (or her) if it is because I am still young at heart or because of more obscure and murky reasons, but I can hardly afford to pay £100 an hour in order to find out. If I had the money, I am not even sure that I would bother. Anyway, Jackie has no grounds to be jealous. Ever since Dorothy left him, Mark has not shown the slightest prurient interest in me.

Finally, there is Mother, of course. With the small inheritance from her own parents, she was able to leave the dark and depressing warren where she had spent most of her life and where she had brought me up. Now, at last, thanks to gas central heating, she can keep warm in winter. The little house she managed to buy has many electrical outlets, so that each of them no longer has to be overloaded with an impressive and dangerous collection of multiple plugs. Faucets do not whine like lambs taken to the slaughter and water pipes are free from the jitters. I try to visit her as often as I can, especially for Sunday dinners. I also take her out shopping or to the cemetery where she loves tending the family tombs.

That's my little world. It is enough to bring some variety into my life. When I am not visiting anyone or cannot find a friend to go out with, I take a bus to the town center and start window-shopping. In spite of my continuing love affair with sewing and clothing design, I buy less and less material because in some hypermarkets, prices of ready-to-wear garments have come down so much that a dress would often cost me more to make from scratch than it does to buy off the peg. With my size ten figure, which has not changed since I was a teenager, I usually don't need any alterations. I also pop into charity shops where, for a couple of quid, it is possible to find, now and then, dresses – some from famous designers – worn only once or twice (or never) by spoiled young ladies from *good* families.

Chapter Eight

1982

Peter and Alma were pedaling on a small country road, a dirt road, barely more than a footpath, winding between bushes of gorse and broom. In spite of his intensely physical job, or perhaps because of it, Peter needed very little rest at weekends and soon felt the urge to "do something." By Sunday afternoon, he was like a lion in a cage and had infected Alma with his interest in cross-country biking. She found it hard to keep up with him. He never went too fast but kept a good ten yards in front of her, if only to ascertain his male superiority. She would lose herself in the contemplation of his powerful muscles. She was desperately in love with her demigod.

On that day, you could hear shotguns being fired fairly close. Alma turned her head in their direction and, with a faint cry, fell off her bike. All Peter heard was the splutter of buckshot thrashing through a hedge and sending debris of vegetation raining all over the road. He braked so hard that he somersaulted over the handlebar. He sprang up and ran towards Alma who, on all four, was howling like a baby. He burst through the hedge, oblivious to scratches from thorns and branches, and just about managed to catch sight of a couple of hunters running away at the other end of the field. "Bastards!" he yelled, shaking his fist.

It goes without saying that they were never found, nor did they have the decency to turn themselves in. The enquiry was conducted with all the slowness and indifference guaranteed to make everyone *forget* the incident. Hunters are above the law. When, to make things worse, they are *local people* who could be *important*, the only conclusion in such a case was that the young lady must have been the victim of "a regrettable and unfortunate set of circumstances."

Alma's howling was turning into raspy, unintelligible, coughing moans. Blood rained from her face onto the surface of the dirt road where she had already left handprints. When she lifted her head, Peter almost fainted. Alma no longer had a face. She looked like a skinned rabbit with dark, liquid holes where the eyes should have been. Without lips, her teeth grinned bright white under an even brighter red film. Bubbles of pink lather sprouted in and out as she breathed painfully through what was left of her nose. Mercifully, she lost consciousness.

Peter remained paralyzed for several minutes, for which he often blamed himself afterwards. He knew there was something that had to be done, something he *must* do. . . but he could not kick-start his brain into action. Eventually, the mental fog started to clear - he should seek help. Not knowing whether Alma was alive or not, he took off his T-shirt and covered her face, then got back on his bike and, as if in a nightmare, pedaled in the direction of the main road where, almost throwing himself in front of a rusty old Fiat, he managed to talk the frightened woman driver to give him a lift to the nearest telephone booth. With trembling fingers, he called 999.

Old Goat   Donatien Moisdon

The sequels of an accident can last for years. That particular accident changed three lives in the long run. Peter, confused, feeling guilty, had to have psychiatric treatment. He recovered but, unfortunately, remained as arrogant as ever. Alma underwent an impressive amount of emergency surgery in order to avoid lead poisoning, followed by plastic surgery. They could not, of course, give her back a couple of eyes. And me? I met Peter.

He had often visited Alma, of course, and admitted that, after each operation, she seemed a little better but for a long time she looked like someone who had been severely burned. When she was allowed home, he could not bring himself to make love to her, although he regretted not being able to do so. The final straw was Alma's steadily deteriorating personality. While some incredible plastic surgery was turning her, once more, into a normal – if blind – young woman, she started to behave in a sulky, irrational and demanding fashion. After a while, Peter gave up.

I was twenty-eight and had spent ten years in the same fashion workshop. One day, out of the blue, I received an invitation to a wedding. They say weddings are the best singles clubs of all, and this one obliged. I had been asked to the ceremony and reception by the electrician who came to our workshop once or twice a year in order to install new outlets, or a second extractor fan or to do some rewiring so that the place would finally comply with every safety standard. The wedding in question was his stepdaughter's. He and I had had coffee breaks together and a few good laughs. He was a remarkably handsome man. He was also very married. In fact, his wife was with him when he drove over to pick me up. Were they taking pity on me?

I enjoyed getting ready. I had designed, cut and made an ankle-length, sleeveless black dress; bareback, but with shoulder straps all the same. My breasts are too small to keep a strapless dress from slipping down the front; small but perfectly shaped, as they say and, above all, firm. That's very important as far as I am concerned. So, I have no complaints in that department. By the time this wedding took place, I had quite given up the idea that I could attract a man; so, when it came to clothes, I simply tried to feel good for my own sake. Same thing with perfumes. I used them sparingly and a bottle of *eau de parfum* would last me more than a year. I haven't changed. Nowadays, I plumb for *Eternity* or *Madame Rochas.* Back then, I went for *Trésor.* Around my neck, I was wearing a thin golden chain that my grandmother had given me when I was still a kid. Nothing on my arms: no bracelet, not even a watch.

I landed among all sorts of people I didn't know. Someone shoved an enormous bunch of flowers in my arms and asked me to take them to the church. I obliged as if I had been in a daze. Drops of water were running down my wrists and a strong whiff of crushed leaves entered my throat and made me choke. The tiny church, apparently dating back to the ninth century, seemed to have sunk within the surrounding tarmac whereas, in fact, as one of the guests explained to me later, the roads, all around it, had been rising steadily.

One had to go down a couple of worn out, permanently damp steps before walking through a side door, all the while careful not to knock your head on the granite lintel. In front of the altar, where I left my flowers, a choir of little girls, all dressed in white, were rehearsing under the baton of an unctuous young priest. Some, arriving late, ran over to take their places and squeezed among the others amidst a warm smell of moist skin, lavender soap and freshly pressed cotton.

Back at the town hall, and having never before met the bride and groom, I shook their hands, voiced my congratulations and decided that I would make the most of what the day had to offer. I was, in particular, hoping that the meal, served in a local hotel, would be enjoyable. I was disappointed. The dining room was grand and overlooking the seashore but, in spite of its huge bay windows, still managed to feel cold and dark. The fact that the walls had been painted Army-green could have had something to do with it. The ceiling seemed as high as that of a church. Penguin-attired waiters moved about with dignified looks on their faces. They kept small, white towels draped over their forearms, and the headwaiter acted like the lugubrious conductor of an orchestra. To make matters worse, the food was only marginally better than the stuff you would normally expect in an old people's home.

The end of the meal was sheer torture. A young oaf of a guest, very loud and very fat, had appointed himself master of ceremonies. He would talk, cajole and even threaten people into standing up and singing something. The more he drank, the more vulgar he became. I felt like a time-traveler back in the days of Thomas Hardy and the crude customs of the countryside, one of which consisted in presenting the bride with a chamber pot full of cider, at the bottom of which a chocolate biscuit imitated a turd to perfection. I could see that some of the guests were happy to regress to that sort of yokelish humour. Others, belonging to a minority of which I was very much a part, became more and more fidgety. Pretending that they had to leave in order to go out for a smoke or simply use the toilet, they gradually and nonchalantly left the room, never to return, even though the wedding cake had not yet arrived.

Sitting in front of me was an extraordinarily attractive young man. We barely exchanged a few words, but I thought I could read in his eyes a certain amusement at the sight of a woman who, on the one hand, was staring at him almost indecently and on the other hand stiffened with embarrassment and disgust as the banquet dragged on. When I left the table, he followed me. We started an inconsequential conversation. I was almost covered with a film of perspiration, and the fresh air of an autumnal afternoon felt wonderful. I knew he shared my opinion of the meal when he declared that he had found it "OK."

"And the wines?" I asked, just to say something. The white had been all right with a first course of cold platter. The red? Simply abominable.

"I don't drink."

"Never?"

"Never."

"Never anything?"

"No: not a drop. No wine, no beer, no brandy, no other drink of any kind."

He did smoke, however; very small cigarettes that he made himself. I gave him time to roll one up, and went on, "Is it because of some religious principle?"

"No, it's just a matter of taste. I've never liked it. By the way, my name is Peter."

"And I am Jane." We both laughed at the association of these two Christian names.

No doubt, if I had to choose between an alcoholic and a teetotaller, I would go for the latter but, as with vegetarians, they make me ill at ease. I cannot help seeing them as insecure people, itching to advertise their differences; differences which, in their minds, are synonymous with *superiority*.

We were less than a hundred yards from the sea. I inhaled with delight the iodine smell of seaweed brought over by a light, cool wind. It had been raining recently. The sun was still hidden behind some clouds, but large patches of blue sky were now stretching over the horizon. Between the flowerbeds and the privet hedges, small sand-drifts had sneaked in during the latest storm.

When you don't have an attractive face; when a good-looking man happens to take an interest in you; when you are so utterly fed up with being a virgin; when you are desperate at the thought that you've never been desired, and also when, instead of believing that "nice girls don't do it," you fully appreciate the value of the right opportunity and how unlikely it is to present itself again. Then, and if you have any brains at all, you make the right decision. While we were walking side by side, I took Peter's hand and squeezed it firmly two or three times. He got the message, stopped, turned towards me, and we kissed. His breath stank of tobacco. I was instantly overwhelmed by an intense feeling of discouragement, and failure. My very first kiss had a taste of. . . prostitution. And yet, with a soldier's grim determination during an assault, I kissed Peter back and accepted a lift. He took me to his caravan.

As in Orpheus' voyage to the underworld, I wanted to discover the unknown and bring back to the surface what should have been my youth; a youth I had fantasized about; a youth which looked like a lovely, laughing, loving and daring teenager. I knew her only too well. She wasn't a dream; she had a body and a face. I had seen her enjoying an orgasm in a room full of overcoats. A few minutes later, I had met her again in a brightly lit kitchen where, smiling and chattering, she had presented me with the picture of a perfectly normal, healthy young lady while making me feel like one of life's rejects.

When I emerged from Peter's caravan, my alter ego Eurydice was still young looking but her eyes were full of sadness and there was a harsh expression on her face.

What I couldn't understand at the start of our relationship was how Peter would manage to make me come. I felt no pleasure under his caresses or his kisses or as he pushed himself into me. Yet, after a minute or so, a tsunami of sensations would crash over me and I would yell, but it was mostly because it took me by surprise. My body was at its peak; it was full of life and energy; it needed orgasms as badly as a plant needs water. Still, I could not help thinking of all those novels I had read, all those films I had seen depicting the delicate ecstasy that we are supposed to experience under the slightest touch from the person we love.

Of course, love – or rather the lack of – was at the heart of the problem. Peter didn't love me, and I didn't love him. Our relationship was physically and anatomically repetitive, but – I kept telling myself – better (oh yes, so much better!) than nothing. I clung to this basic form of sex life like an oyster to a rock. In spite of its brevity and lack of sophistication, what I used to experience during our first few years together was real. No one had ever given me pleasure. What am I saying? No one had **ever** tried. In fact, I was terrified at the thought that Peter could leave me. Luckily (so to speak) he was sentimentally and sexually lazy. He hated surprises, hated *chasing* women (if only because he could not face the possibility of rejection) and he liked nothing better than the monotonous regularity of our meetings.

I don't think he could visualize love as being anything more than the ejaculatory relief of some internal tension.

We did have conversations, however. He often went over Alma's accident. I would listen without interrupting, unwittingly becoming his free psychiatrist. After a while, he stopped mentioning this episode of his life. I was almost sorry about that because I then had to endure the stories of his days as a landscape gardener and his encounters with customers who were invariably stupid while he and his father knew everything and had an answer for every situation under the sun.

Chapter Nine

2002

From my window, I look down at lawns surrounding blocks of flats and the car parks. We are in Autumn. A few russet leaves have landed delicately on the grass. Soon, branches will be denuded, increasing the amount of light reaching the streets on sunny days. A long time ago, I read the biography of a writer who, when she was in junior school, had been asked by the schoolmistress to come up with an essay entitled: *My Favorite Season.* She had chosen: Autumn. What a scandal in that cozy establishment! How could a little girl be so perverse and so defiant as to choose Autumn? All the other pupils had gone for Spring, of course. Summer would have been acceptable. But Autumn? What was the world coming to?

My own junior-school teacher had been more tolerant. When I was ten, I too had been asked to write about my favorite season. I chose Winter, but instead of starting in the expected fashion – "*My favorite season is Winter because..." –* I had written a poem.

<u>Winter</u>

I wait for cold weather to cure our leprosy

and freeze, of all insects, the black, demonic eyes.

When its breath, reddening mountain flanks and valleys,

with a loud sob of joy cleans up the Northern skies,

a blizzard of relief groans through my parted lips.

I close my eyes in peace as Time and the planet

seem to slow down and sleep...

I do wait for Winter to sweep away Madness

and pile it, shivering, on my life's rubbish heap...

Our school mistress was away on sick leave.

Old Goat   Donatien Moisdon

The supply teacher, a nice young man, asked, "Did you write that poem on Winter?"

"Yes, Sir."

"Can you look me in the eyes and say that you actually wrote that poem all by yourself?"

"Yes Sir, I did."

He handed back the exercise book. I hastily looked for a grade but, instead of "A", "B" or "C", he had written "NFC." I managed to be last out of the classroom and asked, "What does NFC mean?"

"Not For Competition." he replied, smiling. Then he added, "As they say at the Cannes Film Festival." He was on playground duty that day and I noticed that he kept staring at me with a puzzled expression on his face, and it made me feel as uneasy as if he had tried to look up my skirt.

I am starting the Winter of my life. All right, forty-eight isn't old nowadays but who, in her right mind, is still expecting Prince

Charming at that age? Winter has swept away madness and illusions. Besides, I have indeed met and known Prince Charming, even if I have lost him. How many women can say that?

Chapter Ten

New Shorter Oxford English Dictionary:

Graceless:

Not in a state of grace, unregenerate; depraved, wicked, ungodly, impious. Also, unseemly, uncouth, improper. Lacking flavour. Merciless, unfeeling, cruel. Pitiless. Lacking charm or elegance.

That's it! That's me, Jane Herner. My face lacks charm and elegance. I am lumbered with graceless features. I've always heard people say so, especially when I was little. Grown-ups would talk in front of me as if I had been deaf or else an animal, a horse for example, at a county fair, "His teeth are too long. What's he got on his knee? Could it be a boil?"

Still, I do have beautiful eyes, they also used to say. . . but my mouth is a little too prominent, like that of a sulking African wood carving. To make things worse, my lips are a little thicker on the right than they are on the left. Consequently, and in spite of years of efforts – efforts I no longer make – I have a tendency to talk through the right side of my mouth. I have been told that all this comes from the fact that my mother's blood group is "A" rhesus negative whereas my fathers was "A" rhesus positive, or something like that. Apparently, I was lucky to have been born at all. Normally, in such cases, there is miscarriage. Is it true? Who will ever know for sure? I must have been twelve or thirteen when I learned all this. For a while, as a child, I often saw myself as a monster and it gave me nightmares.

My body, by contrast, is far from graceless. I wear size ten. Even now, at the venerable age of forty-eight, my breasts are small and firm, my stomach is as flat as a wall, my legs are slim, and my wrists and ankles are delicate. When I left school, I worked in a fashion house. Not one with a famous name but something of a sweatshop, in fact, but we had our own designs, and I was always the one who would climb on a table to conduct fittings. Then, as now, I had the figure for it.

"All right, Jane, let's have a go." someone would yell. I had to drop everything, including my gray smock and the rest of my outer clothing, then hop on a workbench. Wearing only panties – I never had the slightest need for a bra – I was grateful for the change in body position and for an opportunity to rest my fingers and my eyes. Cyril, the only man around, was, as usual, so used to seeing me parading in my underwear that he never displayed the slightest trace of sexual emotion. Standing by the entrance to his office, leaning on the doorframe, his chin in his hand, he seemed only preoccupied with whatever it was that the others were trying to adjust on my shoulders, hips, waist or legs. He calculated the manufacturing cost and estimated his chances of success with retail outlets.

I could have been a top model, earning a fortune, darting around the world in my private jet. The trouble was, I had graceless features - "Not ugly" some people would hasten to add, "No, not ugly. Just a little bit harsh, that's all, and unattractive." Maybe that's why I don't like it when someone wants to take photographs of me, especially in color. Black and white isn't too bad; at least I try to convince myself that it isn't.

Now, I am a cleaner in a junior school. Political correctness hasn't caught up with the likes of me yet. Rubbish men have become *refuse collectors* and black people – at least in the States – have been turned into *African Americans*. What a mouthful! I have yet to meet a white person who gets all hot under the collar for being called White. One of these days, I will probably cease being labeled a cleaner and will be turned into something like a *Floor Technician* or a *School Hygiene Specialist*. I'd much rather they gave me a raise.

I am not a civil servant but enjoy some of their privileges. It would be almost impossible to get rid of me. I'm not proud of that. In order to be fired, I would have to get to work late several days in a row, show up drunk, insult everybody or perhaps parade in the nude in front of the kids. No, I am definitely not proud of my near invulnerability, but I know that I am a failure and, as such, I find a sort of self-satisfaction in reminding myself of job security. It would be damned hard for me to slip through the net.

Talking of nets (hairnets, that is) did I mention that my own hair is – or rather was – jet black? A lovely, deep black, a Chinese woman's black; but it soon turned gray. I dye it now. I experimented with blond, auburn or brown, but it just wasn't me. I went back to black and have not tried anything else for years. I have my hair cut very short and, as it is perfectly straight, it forms a youthful fringe on my forehead. Yes, I did say youthful. When I was young, I looked much older than my years. Now that I am on the verge of being old, people think that I am only in my thirties. As for the hairnet, I wear it at work, of course, to keep the dust away.

I may have the job security enjoyed by civil servants, but I am very low on the salary scale. I also suffer from a bad back, which is not a good thing when you have to wield brooms and mops, carry buckets of water and push vacuum cleaners, floor polishers and other contraptions around corridors and classrooms. My ailment goes back to the days when I was a little girl. I adored gymnastics and am still capable of biting my big toe – not that there is much demand for it – or, when no one is looking, do a somersault on the school trampoline. What they did not tell you, in those days, was that gymnastics could mean severe back pains in later years. I am often in agony but, through a stupid reaction that I cannot explain, I refuse to call in sick. My doctor gives me painkillers and does not seem interested in trying to cure the problem; nor does he have the courage to look me in the eyes and tell me that he can't do anything for me. I clench my teeth and keep going. Sometimes, I let out a deep moan and the other cleaners look at me as if I was a bit strange. Maybe I am. At such moments, the air around me turns gray and every movement makes me feel as if my ankles and wrists are shackled with heavy chains. I become deaf. If asked a straightforward question, I give the wrong answer. My workmates make allowances. I've heard it said, "She's a bit simple, you know" or "She's got a tile missing."

"You will end up as a street sweeper," my teachers used to say, when I was a teenager. They were talking to the boys, of course. At other times it would be, "You'll end up in jail." Everyone laughed but, many years later, I recognised in the local paper the names of three of my classmates who had been caught after a spate of robberies. Our teachers knew, having observed it so many times, that stupidity and irresponsibility are lifetime predicaments. Our so-called Justice has not latched on to this. They turn criminals loose among us almost as soon as they have been tried. Never mind the victims, it gives the Police and the lawyers something to do all over again. . . and again. . . and again. . .

I ended up as a cleaner because I have always failed at everything: gymnastics competitions, school exams. I've only got three GCSEs – or "O"-Levels as they were called then – English, Latin and French. Doggedly, I went on to do "A"-Levels but didn't pass any; and this in spite of the fact that, at school, I always had "As" and "Bs" in my three favorite subjects. Nerves, most likely. Before the Upper-Sixth, I also came home occasionally with a good grade in History but everything else hovered between "D" and "E." I had been labeled an innumerate, which meant that I was also hopeless at physics, chemistry and biology. At night, I would spend so much time on math and science homework that I neglected the rest. How is it then, that if, nowadays, I have the opportunity to watch *Countdown*, I usually get the numbers faster than the two competitors without even having to jot anything down? On the other hand, good as I used to be in English, they regularly beat me at the letters game. If I find a six-letter word, they will find seven. If I find seven, they will find eight, and so on and so forth. As for the conundrum, I don't even try any more.

It is quite tempting to blame someone else for one's own failings. Peter, my first lover, used to do it all the time; but I can't find anyone to blame, not even myself, for I worked conscientiously and with grim determination. It was like fighting ghosts. True, in my first year at Senior School, I did have an English teacher, Miss Toone, who was both nasty and incompetent. With her crooked nose and hunched shoulders, she looked like the witch in Walt Disney's *Snow-white and the Seven Dwarfs.* When, shaking like a leaf, I arrived at the "big school" and turned in my first English essay – something about cruelty to animals, if my memory serves me right – she gave me an "F." As she dropped the exercise book on my desk, she snapped, "Herner" (they called you by your surname in those days) "I want you to look up the word *Plagiarism* in the dictionary. Don't expect to get a grade for someone else's work." It took me several seconds to realize what she meant.

Nowadays I would make a fuss. I would complain to the Head and demand to be given an essay to write all by myself in a classroom, without access to any book but, back then, as a little girl of eleven, I was just stunned. For the rest of the year, and whenever I had English homework, I would just scribble something nonsensical and get another "F." In June, we had "final exams." I did my best, but Miss Toone reluctantly gave me a "C minus." I never had that horrible woman as a teacher for the rest of my school days. From the start of my second year, English grades shot up to "A" and stayed there. My evaluations of the other teachers ranged from "all right" to very good. Most were kind and approachable. Miss Toone was the exception that confirmed the rule.

Nor was there any violence in my school. It was a small, mixed Grammar School, which explains why you could study Latin; my only claim to fame and success had been passing my eleven-plus.

I can't remember any of my schoolmates complaining about being bullied. Discipline was good. There may have been, at times, a background noise of muted conversations in the classrooms or a sudden exchange of funny remarks based on puns or immediate circumstances – as on the day when a teacher pointed to a fat girl chewing gum and shouted, "Debra, in the bin!" and a little voice whined from the back row, "She'll never fit!" – but, on the whole, there were no deliberate attempts at disrupting lessons.

Violence was not very far from our place, though; just down the road, as it happened.

It was called "Mixed Comprehensive," a place where teachers were quite pleased with themselves if they could keep the boys (always the boys, of course) from eviscerating each other; never mind trying to teach them anything. Pupils were convinced they had "received an education" as the media used to put it. The parents had also been cleverly brainwashed into believing so. After a while, even some of the teachers were deluding themselves. There had been talk of rapes and knifings, probably a mixture of truth and teenage exaggeration. Just the same, when, in our school, a boy became a pain in the orifice, our Headmaster would threaten to send him to the nearby Comprehensive. It did the trick.

Our educational establishment was called the Arizona Brickhill Grammar School. In spite of her American-sounding name, Arizona Brickhill had been the first woman in charge of a Port Authority in England, and she was often presented as an example to us girls, especially during morning assemblies. We just called the place Bricks. "Where do you go to school?" "I go to Bricks." "Oh! Fancy that! Posh ennit?" "No, not really." And, in truth, it wasn't. Bricks' catchment area was mostly working class. It was what Grammar Schools had been really and originally designed for, to give children a chance to succeed, regardless of their social status. A chance that I, for one, was not able to grasp. We all liked Bricks. The general atmosphere was very casual – we would say "cool" nowadays – too casual probably because if you could indeed rise to great academic heights, you could also fail miserably in the midst of general indifference from just about everybody.

And the buildings? Awkward question. There were no buildings per se. Bricks was only a loose collection of temporary classrooms scattered on a sort of promontory, a few feet above street level. Even the Head's lair was a Portacabin. Classrooms looked like gray cubes placed on a lake of muddy clay. In each of these cages, the floor shook underfoot, a floor quickly smeared with yellow streaks. In cold weather, electric radiators valiantly wasted the taxpayer's money without noticeably improving the situation. They had an inbuilt fan that would sound like hand-rattles or even death rattles.

Our school fitted in perfectly with the rest of a hastily rebuilt town, complete with dislocated, stony or muddy pavements and the spectacle of permanent and omnipresent construction sites. The whole area had been flattened by German bombers during the war. American tourists regularly asked, "But what happened here? Why all these ruins?" You looked at them as if they were retarded and answered, "Well, the war, of course."

"What war?"

"World War Two, what else?"

"But. . . but. . . that was fifteen years ago!" And that made *you* appear backward in their eyes or, at the very least, like the citizens of a backward environment. They could not have been more wrong, of course, but why waste time explaining?

Old Goat   Donatien Moisdon

The town had a "Business Centre" which looked very much like Brickhill Grammar: cubes of temporary structures for shops and market stalls, but also pubs and, most importantly for me, a subsidized "Working Man's Restaurant." For a derisory amount of money, we ate simple, hearty meals on rough, rectangular, bare, wooden tables for twelve: six people on each side. The cook's best effort remains, in my mind, his beef stew served with boiled potatoes and sprinkled with freeze-dried bits of parsley. When I think back on all this, I do admire the dedication of those who worked in this poor man's eatery. I used to go there as often as my mother's modest income would allow. Of course, you could find many manual workers in that place but there were also low-ranking employees from shops and offices. It wasn't noisy. People – mostly men – ate in near silence and I can recall only one stupid remark. During a sweltering June lunchtime, and while a plump, scarlet-faced waitress was doing her best, rushing among all those tables, a little old man in an outrageously outmoded brown suit with wide lapels and white stripes, looked at her with an inane smile on his face and shouted, "I bet there's froth on that bush of yours" but he was the only one to think it was funny.

In order to go out in the evenings, I had to wait till I was invited. I never had a penny to my name. My mother became a widow the year I was born (my father never set eyes on me). She used to work from home as a seamstress. I can't remember ever being hungry. Often, for our tea, we had a boiled potato, which we would slice and, supreme luxury, eat with a dab of butter on each slice. We thought it was a nice meal.

Every once in a while, school friends would take me to the local café. I ordered a hot chocolate, which I nursed for as long as I dared. The others would start to smoke. I loved that crummy "caff," as they called it, because it was warmer than both school and home. I reached the point when I would inhale with delight its atmosphere of tobacco fumes, wet overcoats, greasy fish-and-chips, malt vinegar and baked beans. Often, I had to fight a strong urge to fall asleep on firm benches covered with crackled red plastic. It spoiled my enjoyment, somewhat.

The only time I was invited to a party, I almost fell asleep also. I was wearing a very fine mauve, long-sleeved, turtleneck, woolen top with, here and there, small white triangles knitted in the material. The trousers, held with a wide golden belt, were in matching mauve but without triangles. Mother and I were so good at sewing and knitting that, with leftover material given away by well-off customers, we used to make all our own clothes. We also hunted for end-of-series sales. Some shops would keep nice things for us, sometimes for free, sometimes at bargain prices. Result: I never looked poor.

That evening, I found the heat rather sleep-inducing but the *coup de grace* was triggered by two glasses of Port gulped in fairly quick succession. I was just about the only one who didn't smoke. You practically needed a compass in order to navigate in the thick fog emanating from all those cigarettes. I danced several times with a lugubrious-looking youngster who wanted to become a doctor and who, a few years later, actually managed to do so. I wasn't attracted to him, and it seemed (but I was no longer surprised) that this lack of attraction was reciprocal. We danced, hugging each other. It was the normal thing to do. It must be said that, in order not to disturb the neighbors, we only played soft music. We also dimmed the lights. I cannot remember the name of that boy and hardly his face. His most intimate gesture was lightly pressing his forehead against mine while the Platters launched into a velvety rendition of *Smoke gets in your eyes*.

I soon felt that I was falling asleep and had to apologize. I withdrew to the room where we had left all our coats. It was the only room in the flat that had no heat. It smelt of cold, wet wool. I turned the light off and lay on one of the two beds. Shivering, I gathered a few coats over myself. It wasn't completely dark: a glass panel had been fitted above the door.

Along with a flash of light and some whispers, the whining of the door hinges woke me up. In walked Dominic, a massive youngster with a brush haircut. He wanted to become an actor but ended up as a stage manager, which is not bad going. He was followed by a girl whom I knew only by sight. I pretended to be asleep, but without shutting my eyelids completely. Hidden under the coats, I was practically invisible. What I could not understand was that Dominic and the girl had not arrived together at the party, or even been dancing together. I was very naïve and quite incapable of imagining that a spark of sensuality could ignite, unexpectedly between two people who knew each other very little or not at all. It was equally possible that they had met before and that there existed between them a discreet and long-lasting complicity.

Dominic closed the door. Standing in the middle of the room, the girl brought her knickers down to her ankles then stepped out of them before shoving them in the pocket of a raincoat (hers, I hoped). She pushed back a few coats and sat on the other bed where Dominic joined her. They kissed. With a quivering heave of her whole body, she uttered a squeak of pleasure when Dominic slid his hand under her skirt. She opened her legs. I could hear some prolonged, deep breathing followed, a few minutes later, by a moan - something like a muffled cry of pain. After a few moments of silence, she helped Dominic undo the zip of his trousers. I had never seen an erect penis before. She grabbed it and rubbed it up and down quite hard, it seemed to me; and I wondered why it didn't hurt. In a very short time, Dominic had come with a couple of grunts; then, shushing each other, the two of them started giggling. They left the room as furtively as they had entered. I now felt wide-awake. I gave them time to go back to the party and, getting up gingerly, turned on the bedside lamp and stared at the streaks of sperm left on the carpet.

Before going back to join the other guests, I made a detour through the toilets in order not to awaken suspicion. When I came out, Dominic was dancing with the girl he had brought in with him and who certainly was not the one he had just taken to the bedroom. As for the latter, there she was, chatting happily with two or three others who had volunteered to do a bit of washing up. The small group headed for the kitchen. My head was on fire. *How could she, how could she?* I felt a bit sick, the double shot of Port playing its part. Were there boys in that room, who looked at me, wondering if I would like to indulge in a quick game of mutual masturbation without giving it any importance whatsoever? I had no boyfriend that night. Silly remark, I never did. In a way, I was glad that I did not have one.

I had been invited by a classmate, and we were in her parents' flat. They were away for the weekend. I decided to join the volunteers for the washing up. In the harsh, neon-tube light of the kitchen, I couldn't help staring at *that* girl. She seemed quite at ease. I knew that, under her short, sleeveless pink dress, she wasn't wearing anything; I knew that Dominic's fingers had just given her an orgasm and that, less than five minutes before, she had made him ejaculate. I was in turmoil. Her name was Janine, as I found out after striking an innocuous conversation with her. I had expected to find her harsh, jaded and vulgar, splattered with make-up and common as muck, but she was not like that at all. She was, in fact, elegant, cheerful, unpretentious and absolutely charming. This unsettled me even more. Her perfect, oval-shaped face with regular features was often lit by an adorable smile. In other words, she did not fit in at all with the way my religious upbringing had depicted girls who *do this kind of thing*. I kept looking at her hands and finally, apologizing to my friends, I decided to go home.

The only other opportunity I had to go out during my upper school years was when some friends took me (quite illegally) in their car to a bar that was rather different from the places I sneaked into from time to time. It was a posh, quiet, club-like, almost silent pub. You could barely make out the muted, soft music. Each cluster of deep red leather seats was separated from other similar clusters by wooden partitions tastefully decorated with reproductions of famous paintings. It created a row of almost private little rooms. You sank so far back and so low in those lovely seats that you had to yank yourself up again, slide your bottom to the edge and stretch your arm out in order to grab your glass from the heavy mock-mahogany table in the center: most uncomfortable, in fact. The smell of the place was rather different from that of my usual cafés. No whiffs of sweaty cloaks, no smoke from cheap cigarettes. Instead, occasional hints of Cognac and Malt Whisky mixed with touches of cigar fumes. As we passed other cubicles, we noticed people drinking Champagne.

On one of the sofas, I saw for the first time two girls kissing. I vaguely knew them. They couldn't have done it in any of my usual haunts. Sexual freedom and tolerance seem to parallel one's standard of living. This was a rich man's place. The depth and softness of the seat had pulled their skirts up and, between their perfect adolescent thighs, I could make out the white triangles of panties. I was overwhelmed by an intense emotion, and I had great difficulty understanding what was happening to me. I was torn between surprise, envy and initial disgust. In those days, I found the idea (the idea only, of course, for I'd had no experience whatsoever) of touching and licking another woman's genitals less hard to accept than the idea of kissing her on the mouth. If no boy ever found me pretty, wouldn't I be well advised to find a girl who might truly love me, and do so to the point of showing it in public? Did it take a lot of courage to "cross over to the other side" and, once there, would I find what I had been craving for? Back in my bedroom, these thoughts trotted in my mind for a long time and kept me awake. At breakfast time Mum asked me why I looked so dreamy and absent-minded.

I did have a boyfriend, so to speak, for a few weeks. Roland was so shy that on the first occasion when he asked if he could walk me home after school, his legs were shaking. I didn't realize to what extent shyness can generate extreme frustration and repressed violence directed against others but also against oneself. Within a few days, he walked me home regularly. Our classmates thought we were going out together. I often wondered, later on, if this had not been the only reason for it all. We were two fragile, frightened creatures who desperately wanted to look as if we were strong and confident; in other words, we wanted to appear as if we fully belonged to the society we lived in.

Once, he invited me to his place. We entered a luxury block of flats with marble floors and silent, modern lifts in the lobby. We went up to the fourth level. Roland opened the door to a magnificent apartment where cream and ochre hues dominated the decoration and where semi-transparent curtains did more than filter sunlight, they insulated the rooms against the harshness of the outside world. There were lovely smells of beeswax, warm cookies and freshly made coffee; but the major surprise, for me, was to meet a maid, a nice young woman, barely older than myself who greeted me with a cheerful "Hello," closed a cupboard door, patted a couple of cushions that didn't need it and added, "All right, Roland, I'm leaving now." I must have looked really dumb; more than dumb: rude, because I was so amazed that I did not answer her smile or her greeting.

As usual, when at someone else's place, I could not help admiring and comparing. Not in a million years would I blame my mother for the lack of comfort in our flat. I knew only too well what her income allowed (or rather did not allow) but I could not help marveling at the sight of a huge fridge; I went into a trance when casting my eyes over thin, central heating radiators along which I would absent-mindedly – or so I pretended – let my fingers slide, in order to "taste" their warmth. I almost cried with sadness when visiting spacious bathrooms and their pastel-colored tiles and faïence, oval bathtubs with shiny taps, and whiffs of fragrant soaps.

At my mother's, we had electric radiators, the most expensive heating system of all. The less money you have, it seems, the more you must pay in order to keep warm. We turned on the heat as little and as rarely as possible. Our tiny kitchen, with wall-cupboard doors that did not close properly and drawers that wobbled and got stuck ajar, had no working surface. We had to peel vegetables and prepare everything else on the table of our equally tiny dining room. In the bathroom, you had to squeeze into the smallest shower cubicle I have ever seen and fight clammy plastic curtains that insisted on wrapping themselves around you. You pulled on a cord and a sort of halo that was supposed to double as a heater would switch itself on, but its function was purely symbolic. In winter, you shivered the whole time while under the shower and even more so when you came out. Nice, long, warm, bubble baths were things we saw in films. Nothing, in our flat, gave the impression of being truly "finished;" we lived for years in what felt like temporary accommodation. Small wonder I almost always stepped gingerly into other people's houses or apartments with, in the pit of my stomach, a painful mixture of relief and frustration.

"Are your parents out?" was the silly question I put to Roland, all the while suspecting that he would not have invited me in if they had been at home.

"I don't have parents. I live with my guardian. He's a nice guy. He is a rep; not often here."

Roland pointed to a seat and chose another one for himself. Terribly self-conscious, he fidgeted for a while then, suddenly inspired, offered an orange juice. I eagerly accepted. For me, it was a luxury. At home it was tap water and like it. As usual, I was far better dressed than my finances would have normally allowed. I was wearing a very fine, knitted, pale-blue top over dark-blue trousers. I drank the orange juice and enjoyed every drop. He was drinking his. I could see that he was starting to fidget. From one minute to the next, I became quite irritable with the whole charade. I got up. He watched me leave with, on his face, an expression of relief that he was not even trying to hide.

The following week, he took me on his small motorcycle to his guardian's second home, only a few miles from our town. For this outing, I had chosen a sort of denim boiler suit, more elegant than the real thing, of course, over a deep red, long-sleeve sweater. We got there in less than fifteen minutes. I had never been on a motorbike and found it exhilarating. Roland had been quite worried. He had urged me several times to lean over with him as he turned right or left, explaining that, at first, some passengers are scared to do so and lean the other way, thus running the risk of getting the bike off balance and creating an accident. I had no problem following the advice and loved it when he went around curves. Sensing that I had immediately adopted the technique, he started to take them faster and faster.

In order to get to the house, you had to climb down a steep footpath carved along a cliff. Roland and I walked on either side of the motorbike, holding it and keeping it from rolling forward. No four-wheel vehicle would have been able to drive through. The place had obviously been built with material brought down on people's backs or in wheelbarrows. It was a charming building, probably dating back to the 1920s, with a small, rather neglected garden on the side. Roland searched his pockets. "Shit" he muttered "I forgot the key."

Supposing he had not forgotten it on purpose, what would have happened? Would he have kissed me? Gone further? Would he have brought me to an orgasm in the way I had witnessed during the party?

Would I have felt, in my hand, his throbbing and spurting erection? Would I have lost my virginity? Leaning against the low wall overlooking the beach, we remained silent. We were all alone in this perfectly secluded garden. There was nothing to keep Roland from kissing me or even – why not? – touching me. I was dying for him to do so but dared not take the first step. Why couldn't I be as free and casual as the girl in the pink dress? I cursed my choice of clothing. I should have put on a skirt instead of this wretched boiler suit.

We went back up the narrow footpath like a couple of culprits, which was exactly what we were: too vain, too shy and too stupid to take advantage of a golden opportunity. I felt like crying and, from the look on his face, so did he but those psychological barriers erected between us by religion, education and prejudice had not yet come down. We'd had at best, a cowardly peek through these barriers for a few minutes but never mustered the willpower to break them open. . . and the moment had passed. With each step I was conscious of a progressively cooling wetness between my legs.

The next day, as we walked along the cemetery wall, on our way back from school, Roland asked, "Would you like to go to the movies with me tomorrow night?" He tried to speak casually but his voice was strained. I did not answer at first. *What*, I reflected sadly, *was the meaning of all this*? We got to the end of the cemetery, at least as far as it skirted the road. Its wall then did a 90-degree angle to the right along a narrow street. I kept thinking of a prank the boys had set up the year before. They had placed a plastic skull on top of the wall, scaring some old biddies shitless.

"No Roland, not tomorrow night."

"Wednesday, then?"

"No, I've got too much work to do."

We stopped walking and faced each other. "Go to Hell!" he suddenly shouted; and, turning round, ran away without looking back, a gray little man in a deserted, gray little street with gray council houses on one side and a gray cemetery wall on the other.

After that, whenever we met, he avoided me and would not talk to me. More than anything, I suppose, he was angry with himself. I had found him good-looking and gentle, but I didn't love him enough to take the first step towards reconciliation. He was a shadow. I needed a boyfriend made of flesh and blood. Nowadays, if he is still alive, I would not mind meeting with him again. We could forgive each other's unsophisticated adolescent behavior. Strange, I feel, the extent to which I still remember him when, in fact, we did not even kiss. He is probably married to a nice girl, has a good job and enjoys an equally good standard of living. All things considered - would I have the courage to admit casually in front of him that I ended up as a school cleaner?

I was twenty-eight years old when I finally made a more complete and gratifying acquaintance. As years went by, I had realized that teenagers – and even young men – were not terribly interested in elegant figures. There are exceptions, of course, but generally speaking, what they want, above all, are lovely faces. It is only with the passing of time that dirty old men – or true worshippers of Eros – learn how to appreciate the hidden charms of slim women burdened with unattractive features. Maybe that's why I had to wait for such a long time before I met my first lover.

Chapter Eleven

1993

Late May. Warm evening. Gray skies. Not a whiff of wind. Columns of insects dancing up and down by the lilac tree and, from time to time, the melancholy whistling of a blackbird hidden in the vegetation. It underlined the meditative stillness of the moment. Lawrence and I had finished our dinner but, as the days were getting longer, we had drifted towards the patio. We were lying down on deck chairs and had allowed ourselves to become hypnotized by the near silence of the garden; also, by its fragrance of young leaves and flowers thirsting for evening dew. . . And to think that some people cannot go anywhere, or do anything, without pop music blaring in the background!

Lawrence and I often had long conversations. He would introduce me to pieces of classical music I didn't even know existed: Haydn's operas or Gustav Mahler's symphonies, for example. It must be said that the quality of his magnificent hi-fi was miles above that of my ghetto blaster. I, on the other hand, had made him discover Hector Berlioz's *Le Spectre de la Rose* sung by Janet Baker. Those few minutes of enchantment, descending from a world that is not ours, a paradise lost perhaps, would often make me cry. Peter would have been completely incapable of understanding these things. My former lover reminded me of Pluto, so remote from the sun's warmth and light that one of its years lasts as long as 242 of ours.

In most circumstances, whether in front of the fireplace or on the patio, Lawrence and I did not talk. I had found Peter's silence irritating because it betrayed his incapacity to say anything of interest. Peter was an empty warehouse. By contrast, I used to find Lawrence's silence soothing and comfortable. It wasn't the same sort of silence: his was the silence of a person who had sensitivity and culture; the silence of a warehouse crammed to the roof with fascinating objects. I found it reassuring. At times like these, life flowed through me drop by drop, second by second, distilling sensations which, for lack of a better word,

Old Goat — Donatien Moisdon

I would have to call: happiness. Lawrence's voice yanked me out of my reverie.

"Apart from helicopters, no one can see us here, between these walls. When it's very hot, I sunbathe in the nude."

I didn't know what to say, therefore said nothing, but I tried to visualize what he must look like, in the altogether, on his deck chair. Not very exciting. Was he expecting me to join him? Oddly enough, I felt that it would not have bothered me in the least; on the one hand, he had already seen me in a monokini, and, on the other hand, I just knew, somehow, that I could trust him. I even came to wish that, weather permitting, he would broach the subject again.

In any event, the weather, that evening, decided that the garden needed water. I was wearing a white shirt tucked in mouse-coloured trousers and I could see, on my thighs, the dark spots created by the first drops of rain. Lawrence and I beat a hasty retreat. The dogs followed. Back in the dining room, we left the French doors wide open and remained for several minutes, just gazing at the rain and breathing in its fragrance of freshly awakened earth. Every thirty seconds or so, the blackbird kept whistling as if nothing much was happening. Suddenly, the gentle rain turned into a downpour, filling the whole garden with its powerful hissing, making every leaf flutter in a panic. The edges of the garden shed allowed curtains of water to splash down noisily onto the pavement. I badly wanted to cock my head to one side and let it rest on Lawrence's shoulder. He may have felt something of the kind himself because, after he had called for a taxi and helped me put on my raincoat, he said, very softly, "I'd like to hold you in my arms."

Instinctively, stupidly, I took a step back. I have often reflected afterwards on what happened at that moment and I still don't understand what made me react as if, somehow, a hug from Lawrence was a revolting and disgusting prospect. I mentioned it to him later. He said that before making his request, and in order not to frighten me, he had waited until I was wrapped in my raincoat. That way, he thought, I would feel less vulnerable. Such old-fashioned consideration was typical of Lawrence. Back then, like a scolded child, he had muttered, "You are coming back next Wednesday, aren't you?"

"Of course. . . if you want me to. . ."

He just smiled. At home, stretched on my bed with all my clothes on, I clearly visualized and understood for the first time to what extent I would have missed these wonderful Wednesdays. They had become windows onto a world which was not mine but which I craved. Lawrence had told me of a similar experience while he was in basic training at the start of his National Service. This awareness of another world had had a profound effect on him.

He and several coach loads of raw recruits had ended up in gloomy barracks that were dirty green on the outside, dirty beige inside. No matter how often or how hard these buildings were scrubbed, they still looked dirty. He found himself in the same room as nineteen other young men, none of whom were particularly nasty, aggressive or stupid, but they were illiterate or semi-illiterate. Their tunnel vision of life led them to rather sterile conversations. Friendships were impossible. They only reacted to remarks about football, birds (not the feathered kind), memorable drinking sessions and pranks. The non-coms were far worse: a collection of alcoholics, unpredictable, sadistic human failures. Officers were strictly for inspections and parades. What did they do the rest of the time?

Lawrence accepted all this without question. He was keenly aware of the fact that, at any given moment, a great many people were suffering more than he was. He knew his ordeal would not last. One day, almost by accident, he'd pushed open the door to the chaplain's trailer, a long room with a long table, used for meetings of the rare churchgoers in the boot camp. It was empty. It smelled of warm wood and dusty paper. Shelves were full of worn-out magazines and detective novels. Next to one of the windows, there stood an old-fashioned record player and a pile of records. Lawrence pulled one out at random: Bach's third Brandenburg Concerto. He placed it on the turntable and got it going. Then, just as it happens that a sudden stomach heave can make you throw up before you even realize what is going on, Lawrence felt tears running down his cheeks. He looked out of the window, surveyed the dark, menacing line of fir-trees surrounding the compound, and all of a sudden, became keenly and painfully aware that behind this forbidding frontier and beyond this place where men kept milling around like ants without actually achieving very much, there really existed something called Civilisation. Afterwards, Lawrence did not go back to the chaplain's room, nor did he ever meet the chaplain himself.

Lawrence's house, real as it was for me, had nevertheless become the symbol of an inaccessible "beyond." Not going back there would have felt like being sent into exile. "The old geezer's got the hots for you." Peter had said dozens of times. Why had I refused to admit it? What was I afraid of? The differences in our ages? No, of course not. I was afraid of myself, afraid of not knowing how to react or how to behave; afraid of losing his friendship (his love?).

The following Wednesday, I kept almost silent the whole time. I was ashamed and also, of course, apprehensive of saying anything wrong. Lawrence completely misunderstood. He thought I was sulking. I tried to reassure him, but my throat was tight, and I sounded as if I was lying. He must have taken it badly because, when I asked to go home earlier than usual, he did not object. I was desperate. *I'm losing him and it's all my fault,* I kept thinking. *He probably thinks it's HIS fault. I've got to do something.*

I had always gone to his house on a Wednesday, never on any other day. On the Sunday of that week, I did something quite extraordinary. I still don't understand how it happened. I would like to be able to say that it was all planned, all laid out, like the tactics of a great general but it was not. I let myself be guided by instinct. . . or else, my brain had been scheming without telling me. Whatever the reason, I could feel, within myself, on that particular Sunday morning, an irresistible strength. I was possessed, as one who had been taken over by an extraterrestrial being (I should stop watching science-fiction on TV).

For a while now, Lawrence had gone back to learning French. He didn't do things by half: twenty minutes every morning with a self-teaching book, the news from *TV Liberté* recorded every day, then replayed in loop on his car radio, a CD-ROM for his computer and a subscription to the magazine *Science et Vie*. He was making remarkable progress.

To begin with, he had asked for my help. I dredged what remained of my schoolgirl French and was able to help him, but he soon overtook me, leaving me panting far behind. The clever clogs had even started reading full-length children's stories in the original language.

Around eleven o'clock, I stretched my hand towards the telephone. I had never called Lawrence, and he had never called me. I dialed. Suddenly, I was scared that it might be answered by a lady friend he had *forgotten* to mention. Too late: it was ringing. He answered almost immediately, "Drover speaking." His voice was polite but firm and much more businesslike than I had anticipated. Now, I was really scared.

"Lawrence, it's me."

"What a pleasant surprise!"

I was instantly relieved. His voice seemed, at once, full of warmth and sunshine. I went on, "Could you help me translate a sentence into French?"

"I'll try."

"OK, there it is, 'I feel like making love to you.'"

"No problem. 'J'ai envie de faire l'amour avec toi.'"

I repeated slowly, "J'ai envie de faire l'amour avec toi."

"That's it, you've got it."

A long silence was now spreading between us. I was only conscious of our breathing. It sounded like the wavelets of a rising tide whispering on a sloping beach. I said again, insisting on each word and separating them clearly, "Lawrence – j'ai – envie – de – faire – l'amour – avec – toi."

"Oh, my God!" Another long silence. Then, with his voice choked with emotion, he added, "I'm sending a taxi."

"No rush. Give me an hour or so."

"All right, then. I'll send a taxi in an hour's time."

He told me later that he had experienced a moment of sheer panic, not only at the idea of making love to me, but also because, on Sundays, his housekeeper did not come around. Dirty dishes had piled up on the kitchen counter, his bed wasn't made and he, himself, still in his dressing gown, had not yet showered or shaved. He rushed to the bathroom and, in order to gain some time, exceptionally used an electric shaver.

Then, hastily dressed, he had frantically started tidying up the place.

Unaware of all this feverish activity, I also had a shower, and also shaved. Only in my case, it meant refreshing armpits and pubis. I wanted to be perfect for him. I casually chose a long-sleeved, turtleneck, pale-green sweater over ivory-coloured trousers. For underwear, I plumbed for a very innocent-looking and simple pair of white panties. No bra, of course. Behind my ears and on my wrists, I dabbed a few drops of a very expensive perfume Lawrence had given me, and which I had almost never worn.

As I arrived at his place, and as I crossed the front garden and petted the dogs, I felt completely calm and relaxed, and quite amazed that it should be so. I had expected to be a nervous wreck. Lawrence opened the door. His hair was still wet. We went to the living room, and he took me gently in his arms. Only then did I feel a bit awkward and started wondering how I should behave. Where was his bedroom? I had never been there.

At any rate, we stayed downstairs. He kissed me, slid his hands under my sweater and took it off gently. He was kissing as I had never been kissed before. His lips conveyed an incredible feeling of subtlety: an unexpected mixture of softness and urgency; the most delicate sensuality I had ever experienced. His first kiss, like all those that followed, was long, very long. Lawrence did not give the impression that he was keen to move on to something else. He savored the moment and made it last. He pushed me back at arm's length and, eyes shining, looked at me intensely, "You are. . . so. . . so beautiful!"

"You've already seen my breasts at the workshop."

"I wasn't talking about your breasts."

I knew my breasts were firm, very small and young-looking, and I was quite confident about that, but if Lawrence wasn't talking about my body, what could he possibly mean? "Are you making fun of me?" I whispered.

"You silly goose: I am desperately in love with you. Don't tell me you didn't know."

"I didn't want to know. . . too scared to get hurt, I suppose."

All the while, he stroked my chest and the sensations he was giving me were so fresh and so intense that I closed my eyes and moaned. His hands were wonderfully warm and soft. It was as if no one had ever touched me before; and, in a way, no one had. No one had loved me and touched me at the same time. Perfect pleasure can only arise if both body and soul are being loved equally. For the first time in years, my panties were getting soaked. It felt as if I had peed in them, and it made me laugh. "What's the joke?" asked Lawrence with a touch of uneasiness in his voice.

"No joke: I am simply very happy and . . . I have just understood a lot of things. I'll explain later." I sat on the couch where, lovingly, Lawrence finished undressing me. He managed to do several things at the same time: take off my trousers, my socks and underwear while undressing himself, kissing me from head to foot and marveling at every detail of my body. I was panting; I had an urgent and painful need to feel him inside me and waited for him to come in, but instead, he knelt in front of me and started to lick my labia and clitoris. Meanwhile, his hands were roving from my knees to my breasts. I was diving into a new dimension made of warm, wet, light, gentle, strong sensations - a maelstrom of contradictions. Far, far away, I could hear someone yelling. It was I.

When I bobbed up to the surface, I was still in the same position. Between my legs emerged the smiling face of my dear old Goat, which had now become the most beautiful face in the world. Still shivering with remnants of pleasure, like a building tottering in the aftermath of an earthquake, I gazed at Lawrence and wondered if I had ever properly looked at him before. His voice startled me, "Why," he was asking, "did you cry 'no, no!' when you came? Did you want me to stop?"

"I can't remember saying 'no' and you certainly didn't hurt me. Maybe it was because I just couldn't believe what was happening to me."

"Don't tell me it's the first time someone did that to you?"

"Oh, Lawrence, if you only knew! Believe me if I tell you that I have just lost one of my virginities and I'm sure I have many more to go. . . Don't you want to. . ." I didn't know how to finish my sentence without sounding clinical, or vulgar, but he knew what I meant.

"Give me a minute. Let me admire your beautiful flower. . . its petals, all pink and swollen." With the tips of his fingers, he then traced a line on the ridge which, starting from the groin, divides the thigh into two concave expanses, one towards the buttocks and the other towards the top, a ridge as taut as a violin string when legs are wide open. "Do you know the name of this long muscle?" he asked.

"No idea, but surely it's not a muscle, it's a tendon."

"No, it's a muscle, a very thin muscle - to my mind, one of the most beautiful details of female anatomy."

"And it's called?"

"The tailor's muscle. How appropriate for a seamstress! You have the longest, softest, smoothest tailor's muscle I have ever seen. I worship it." and he kept sliding his lips and his tongue from one side to the other of the ridge while I basked in his admiration. I felt so light, so immaterial, so perfect! I managed to ask, "And what is the second most beautiful detail?"

"There is no second best with you. Wherever I look, I think it's the most beautiful part of you. Your thighs, for instance, drive me insane." He illustrated his insanity by brushing them with his fingers then kissing them from knee to groin and finally placing his mouth back on my clitoris.

I know it's hard to believe but I didn't know that a woman could have two or more orgasms in a row. When Lawrence started licking me again, I thought it would be painful, but of course, it wasn't. At some point, he stopped, opened my inner lips as wide as he could and blew, as he would have on a spoonful of hot liquid. I marveled at the unexpectedly delicious freshness. I closed my eyes and let myself sink in that newfound world of pleasure. Lawrence was an artist. His tongue was going up and down, of course, but also from side to side and, above all, in circles. . . slow, exasperatingly slow, wonderful circles which, at times, pushed the little hood of the clitoris completely out of the way. I indulged in deep, throaty moans of delightful frustration then, after a length of time that seemed both short and long, I exploded anew.

Vaguely aware that my buttocks were sliding in a mixture of saliva and vaginal secretions, I rested my nape on the back of the couch and tried to catch my breath. Lawrence finally penetrated me. Always the gentleman, he supported himself, one arm on each side of my head. I barely felt what he was doing but became suddenly conscious of the gentle warmth of his sperm spreading inside me.

There are probably as many forms of love as there are couples and individuals. If, after that first real encounter between Lawrence and me, I had been asked to describe our relationship in one word, I would have said *dependency.* I could not do without him anymore. As with a fast drug, I had become an instant addict. Fortunately, I was keenly aware of this addiction and quite determined not to wear out Lawrence's patience by sticking to him like a leech, twenty-four hours a day, however much I may have felt like doing so.

The weeks that followed were without a doubt the happiest in my whole life. I did not move in with Lawrence. We had both agreed on this. Beyond the fact that I did not want to crowd him, I had no wish to give my mother the feeling that I no longer needed her. She who, from the start, had been very much against my affair with Peter, was now glad to see how happy I was. Like so many people of her generation, she was beginning to realize that the sort of morality taught by Catholic priests was nothing but a long list of sexual prohibitions whereas true morality, based on respect for others and personal righteousness was not considered terribly important. Mum was still a good Christian; she went to mass every Sunday, but she had learned all by herself something the clergy had always been so careful not to preach: tolerance.

I may not have moved in with Lawrence, but I spent many wonderful days and nights at his place. I was very shy the first time we went up to his bedroom, but it turned out to be an ordinary bedroom: big and high-ceilinged (as were all those late 19th century designs) yet ordinary just the same. There was a large, plain, double bed, very high off the floor but otherwise not unusual in look or style, an old television sitting on a chest-of-drawers in a corner, a couple of cane chairs, wallpaper painted with quaint, bucolic scenes in Staffordshire blue and, most surprising of all, shelf after shelf straining under the weight of hundreds of strip-cartoon books. There was also an impressive collection of VHS tapes. I pulled one out at random: it was a pornographic video devoted to female masturbation. Lawrence was looking at me with a silly smile on his face. "I am not ashamed to have porn videos, you know; and I am not ashamed to say that I sometimes masturbate while watching them." And he added with a note of hope in his voice, "I just love watching a woman making herself come."

"I wouldn't mind watching a man playing with himself. . ."

Misty with emotion, passion and sheer lust, our eyes locked for a while; then Lawrence kissed me and, with his lips moving against mine, whispered, "What a wonderful journey we are starting together!"

Indeed, it turned out to be a wonderful and endless journey. I thought discovery had its limits, but I was wrong. After all, with only seven notes on the musical scale, the contemporaries of Vivaldi and Telemann were probably convinced that there was not much else that could be discovered in music, and that composers would be bound to plagiarize themselves, or each other, forever; then came Mozart, Beethoven, Brahms, Verdi, Berlioz, Bruch and so many more. With seven notes you can reach infinity. With a body, (and as soon as you can ban modesty and hang-ups, in other words as soon as you never say "no" to the person you love) you can reach infinity. A whole life would not exhaust the possibilities and variations in a relationship, especially for those people who, like golden needles lost in a haystack of Mediocrity, truly love each other. They die happy to have always dared.

Getting used to an honest-to-God lover after knowing only a conceited young stud was exhilarating and liberating but not always easy. Like most women of my generation, I thought I had seen, read and understood everything there was to see, read and understand about sex. I was sure that nothing could possibly surprise or shock me. There were moments, however, when some of Lawrence's suggestions (requests, never demands) would make me gasp, and I would be tempted to turn them down. With hindsight, I am so glad that I kept sailing in his vessel like the adoring crew member that I was! I would be even more unhappy now if I had to admit, *I could have. . . I should have. . .*

I also had to adapt to Lawrence's non-sexual habits. During the first night I spent with him, I went to the loo, then came back to bed gently and silently so as not to disturb him. I took great care not to touch him, and to leave a couple of inches between us while I went back to sleep. To me, it was the thing to do. I had been trained by Peter, who was never in the best of moods when you woke him. He acted like an Oriental potentate. *How dare you wake the heir to the throne, Prince Ahmed Salafumal, in the middle of the night?* Excellent opportunity for him to assert his authority and put down his female with a few, well-felt grumbles.

At breakfast time, Lawrence asked casually, "Do you find me repulsive?" He must have seen, by the expression on my face, and the progress of a croissant frozen between my cup and my mouth, that I had no idea what he was talking about. He went on, "You got up during the night but when you came back to bed you avoided me."

"I didn't want to wake you up."

"Is that all?"

"Of course, that's all. Would you rather I had disturbed you?"

"You did wake me up or I wouldn't ask the question, but I expected you to snuggle up to me. I love the surprise of a hug during the night."

"No problem next time."

We were smiling by then, having avoided what could have been our first fight. There never was another, not even close. I was so relieved that my neck, ears and lips suddenly felt very hot and red. Almost out of breath, I grabbed Lawrence's hand over the table and stammered, "I'll give you that hug right now if you want."

"Oh, Jane, I find it so exciting when you take the initiative!"

We were both in dressing gowns. In the second that followed, we were without dressing gowns and ran towards the staircase. An hour later, and after another orgasm (mine, as the poor darling had exhausted his reserves during the night) followed by a little nap, I woke up against the warmth of Lawrence's body and mumbled, "We knew each other for almost a year before we had sex. Most men would have been discouraged by the third date. Why were you so patient with me?"

"I thought that for as long as she accepts my invitations, I have a chance."

"Nothing more?"

"Nothing more to start with. Then I gradually fell in love and, as weeks and months went by, I got really scared, thinking that I might never get to sleep with you."

"I have been so cruel. . . but without meaning to."

"And I believed you cared for Peter."

"Peter is a bad memory. He represents a period in my life I am not proud of, and, for that, I blame only myself. I don't bear any grudge against him. He is what he is, and it would be easy to find far worse. Brutal, beer-swilling morons are two a penny. He is none of that." I propped myself on an elbow and looked deep in Lawrence's eyes, "What would you have done if, after leaving Peter, I had started going out with another man?"

"I would have kept inviting you. I would have said to myself: let her meet two or three selfish, macho cretins; sooner or later, she'll be able to see them for what they are."

"You seem very sure of yourself."

"Hardly. I would have been a nervous wreck. So many men manage to keep women they don't deserve! They bank on the girls' low self-esteem and fear of being left alone. It would have led me to a diet of wishful thinking and hope: two of the worst poisons concocted by our modern way of life."

On that particular morning, the breakfast table was not cleared before midday.

Chapter Twelve

Stretched out on chaise longues, we were naked behind the house. Lawrence's body was not as ugly as I had feared. Yes, he could have lost a few pounds which had treacherously accumulated around his waist but, in spite of his slight claudication, he had strong legs and powerful shoulders. His chest was smooth, which I greatly appreciated. I hate body hair and would have found it impossible, however much I was in love, to sleep with a man who was reminding me of an orangutan; not that I ever tried giving a hug to an orangutan. Lawrence looked so neat and so clean! I don't mean "clean" as in "personal hygiene;" I just mean that "clean" is the best word that comes to mind when describing his body. I always felt like brushing my fingers against that chest of his, kissing it and going down until I caught his penis between my lips, even when, all excitement gone, all desire exhausted, neither of us could have started making love again.

"Stroking a man's chest feels so good!" I had whispered to him one morning when he was half asleep.

"Wouldn't know," he mumbled. "Never tried." This cost him a few gentle punches while we both burst into silent laughter.

It was nine o'clock in the morning. Butterflies nonchalantly explored the buddleias. That particular Sunday promised to be a scorcher. Protected, as it was, by high walls on two sides and by the house behind, Lawrence's patio did not receive a single breath of wind. In my nostrils and the back of my throat I could smell and taste the last traces of the previous night's dampness lingering on flowers, but the air itself was already dry; so dry that Lawrence and I did not perspire. Blackbird whistling had been replaced by pigeon coos and the strident insistence of a single cricket. Sprawled on the coolness of the sandstone, Pyrrhus and Xenophon had found a patch of shade. From time to time, they sighed deeply while opening an eyelid just to make sure everything was all right.

I became lost in the contemplation of my stomach, so flat, so lyrically celebrated by Lawrence with, at the end, the gentle bulge of the pubic area that I always kept impeccably depilated. Further away, my looks lingered on those thighs that still drove Lawrence quite insane.

The sun seemed to be spreading a delicate sheet of sandpaper on my skin, and I knew I would soon have to move back into the house or seek the protection of a parasol, but I was too lazy to set it up. Above all I did not want to disturb Lawrence. His voice made me jump, and I was grateful for it. While wondering whether or not I should retreat from the sun, I was, in fact, dozing off and in danger of burning to a crisp.

"Working tomorrow?" he asked in a falsely casual tone.

"Of course. Tomorrow is Monday."

"Mmmm. . ."

I knew him well enough, by then, to sense that he had something on his mind. Every time he broached an important topic, he started with an innocent-sounding question, then added, "Mmmm. . ." and remained silent for a while. I got up. Lawrence turned his head towards me, "You going in?"

"Yes, I better. . . I think."

"I'm going with you."

"I'll put something on."

I went back up to the bedroom. I had left my clothes on the floor. Very few articles of clothing indeed: two to be precise. There was a tiny pair of white panties that I had worn only a few hours the day before and an adorable, very short, sleeveless, pale yellow dress with golden buttons on one side. I had arrived barefoot in sandals. We'd had twenty-nine degrees in the shade all week, and the forecast was the same for the next few days. Lawrence watched me slip into the dress with as much fascination as he would have if I had taken it off. Whenever he said, "I worship you," I believed him. The mouth can lie, not the eyes.

"Lawrence," I said to him one day, "don't put me on a pedestal."

"Why not? That way, I can look up your skirt."

But he was very serious now. Sitting on the side of the bed, he seemed oblivious to the fact that he was still stark naked. He stared at the carpet and looked like a rattled little boy who had done something wrong and is about to confess. I kneeled on the bed behind him, put my arms around him and rested my head on his left shoulder. "Something wrong?"

"How would you like to stop spending your days in that sweatshop of yours?"

"I wouldn't. What would I do?"

"You could marry me."

I think I know how people react when told they've won the lottery. They can hear the words. They understand what they mean. It all makes sense, but it does not sink in. Recently, I had, of course, fantasized about sharing my life with Lawrence in this magnificent house; but it had remained a dream, as inaccessible as wishing to have been born something else: an Egyptian princess under Rameses II, for instance or a famous violinist. I jerked back, then moved to sit next to Lawrence while hiding my face in my hands. He curved an arm over my shoulders and whispered, "You don't seem to like the idea."

I removed my hands which, by then, were shaking and placed them firmly on my knees. I could see myself, looking haggard, in the full-length mirror of the main wardrobe, then the reflection became fuzzy - and I woke up, lying on the bed. It was dark. Lawrence had closed the drapes. I could see a thin line of light at the top and feel a wet flannel on my forehead.

"How do you feel?" he asked softly.

"Fine. What happened?"

"You fainted, darling. The doctor is on his way."

And then I remembered. By now, Lawrence had got dressed and was wearing long, black Bermuda shorts and a pale-green T-shirt. I looked at him intensely.

"No need for a doctor, Lawrence. Did. . . did I hear you correctly, just now?"

"You heard right - I asked you to marry me."

If I had not been already lying down, I would probably have fainted again. I could feel tears streaming down my cheeks. My chest hurt. My whole body was twisted in agony. To try coping with this unbearable pain, I started howling like a wolf: a long "Aaaaaoooouuh" followed by another and another. I could not stop. Whipped into a frenzy, Pyrrhus and Xenophon, downstairs, started howling as well. Then someone rang the bell, and the dogs went absolutely wild.

Old Goat   Donatien Moisdon

I heard the fall of an armchair they must have knocked down. Somehow panicking, Lawrence was trying to free himself since, without realizing, I had grabbed his wrist and squeezed as hard as I could. He managed to pry his arm off.

A few minutes later, a tall, young and handsome doctor came into the room. I started laughing hysterically - how could I be receptive to this man's charm when I was, at the same time, ecstatic at the idea of marrying Lawrence? My electrical circuits had, it seemed, interfered with each other and tripped a switch somewhere. I felt like a computer, scanning its programmes without finding what it's looking for, then doing nonsensical things, and finally heading for a crash. As I kept laughing, I could read, as if on a screen: *your software's gone wild.* I wanted to shout, "I can see two. . . I am doing, thinking. . . two things at once." But, inside, I was only a mess of erratic pulses hitting and bouncing off the black partitions of my brain or a swarm of painful pebbles ricocheting on virtual bodies of water. No words came out, except that my laughter changed into a raucous sound reminiscent of death rattles. I got very, very scared.

I saw the doctor whisper something in Lawrence's ear and could make out that he was mentioning drugs. Lawrence smiled and shook his head. Temperature. . . blood pressure. . . a light shoved in my eyes. . . a shot in the shoulder. . . I went out like a light.

Around four p.m. I woke up with a sensation of dust in my mouth. The drapes were still pulled shut. Silence. . . disturbed only by the buzz of a fly caught between the window and the net curtains, no bird song from the garden. Even the cricket had shut up, but I could feel that the weather was still glorious. I was alone. I tried to get back to sleep even though I was dying for a glass of water and a pee. What on earth had happened to me?

Not so long ago, some people still believed that you could be possessed by the Devil or, at least, by one of his underlings. An exorcist was solemnly brought over and started the ceremony with his mumbo-jumbo and theatrical gestures. The evil spirit would then leave the victim's body and, in the process, make him (or her) howl and writhe sensationally. Spectators were most impressed. In the end, bone tired and in tears, the poor sod would collapse and calm down. That is roughly what had just happened to me.

It was as if a toxin, stored within my body for decades, had just escaped through every pore of my skin, leaving me exhausted, limp, covered in sweat but purified and pacified. I could smell that toxin: it permeated the whole bedroom and made the bed reek with a strong, peppery, wild odor not unlike that of a skunk. I got up and took everything off. I threw my dress and panties in the linen basket without worrying about going home; I added the bed sheets. I then headed for the loo where I urinated with relief, or rather with delight; a long, strong, noisy, smelly pee which carried out the rest of my inner poison.

Old Goat   Donatien Moisdon

Ever since I was a child, I had suffered from having graceless features, from being, not just Jane, but "Plain Jane," as they say. I had suffered far more than I was willing to admit. Only now did I realize how much anguish I had been repressing. Poison had accumulated without my knowledge, or perhaps I just did not want to know. After all, you have to go on living, don't you? A great many people harbored more reasons than I did for being unhappy. In spite of my bad back, I was in very good health. In spite of my low income, I wasn't unemployed. I didn't starve; I had a roof over my head. In the morning, I didn't have to leave the apartment and walk to work with butterflies of fear and frustration in my stomach, expecting to be mocked, insulted or threatened, a situation familiar to many teachers, prison wardens or policemen (and women) every day. I liked the atmosphere of the workshop, even if its routine was often hard and monotonous. Cyril was always fair; he never harassed any of us, either sexually or to *encourage* someone to leave. The girls were companionable. Besides, as their top model, was I not, in a way, the star of the show? *Do reflect, you silly woman, on all those who suffer twenty-four hours a day, cancer-ridden, bed-ridden, paraplegic or worse. Have enough decency not to make a fuss about the fact that you don't look like Heather Locklear, Elizabeth Montgomery, Jenna Elfman or Mary Tyler More. In this wretched world of ours, and by most people's standards, you should be happy.* Thus, had I managed to convince myself. For years and years, this constant lie had poisoned my heart.

An evil spirit had now left me. I could walk with my head held high: I was beautiful. Not just pretty but beautiful, which is much better, I think. I flushed the toilet and, along with that crucial pee, down went a lifetime of inhibition and shame. On hearing the rush of water, Lawrence ran up the stairs and into the bathroom. He found me ready to step under the shower and took me in his arms. I rested my forehead on his shoulder. My hair was stuck on my brows and nape. Perspiration burned my eyelids, dripped from my nose, rolled between my breasts and flowed down my armpits. "Oh, Lawrence, I stink." He did not answer for a while, being content to rock me slowly, as if I had been a baby, his big hands sliding on the sweat on my back. Finally, he pushed me away gently and looked me in the eyes, "You still haven't given me an answer. Will you marry me?" I felt tears welling in my eyes and nodded as I buried my head in his neck once again. It then occurred to me that he deserved a better reply. I placed my lips against his ear and pronounced clearly, "Yes, I want to marry you." He squeezed me harder against him and, to my surprise, I realized that he too was now crying. "I've been waiting all my life for such an incredible moment of happiness," he whispered.

Later, Lawrence had to drive over to my mother's in order to bring back something for me to wear. I never asked what sort of explanation he gave her. While he was away, I took a shower, shampooed, then went down to the kitchen where I drank two tumblers of orange juice, one after the other. Back in the bedroom, I borrowed Lawrence's hair dryer. Every morning, he would lovingly dry and fluff up his lovely white hair until it looked like a collection of overlapping shells. The first time I saw him doing this, I was quite amused. It had never occurred to me that men could use hair dryers. You learn something every day. With my head now dry, I put clean sheets on the bed and lay on top, arms and legs stretched out, so as to bask in the mildly lavender-scented freshness of Irish linen.

I heard Lawrence come home. Yes, from now on, I could think and say *home*. What an exhilarating feeling! I realized that I seemed to be floating over the bed, as in those near-death experiences one reads about in magazines. First, I was aware of the plaintive squeak of the gate's hinges, then the tires of his car crushing the gravel in the front garden. The dogs were whining in anticipation as if they had not seen him for weeks. The front door opened, and finally Lawrence's heavy footsteps went up the staircase; and I wondered how many hundreds. . . how many thousands of times I would hear these sounds, all laden with a promise of love, tenderness and reassurance.

Lawrence stopped at the bedroom door and gazed at my naked body. My labia had swollen to the point when they became almost painful, and he surely noticed. He held out a pair of pale-blue knickers and a white, short-sleeved dress with faded, sepia drawings of Tower Bridge on it. "Will that be all right?" I just smiled. He went on, "Your mother cried when I told her." He was staying at the door, almost as if he had been too shy to come into the room. I barely heard what he said. I could only think of offering myself to the admiration, the touch, the kisses, the love of this wonderful man. It was indeed like a near-death experience; no, come to think of it, it was more like a real death: that of the old Jane. It was also the birth of a new one, a translation from darkness into light, from stress into comfort, from limbo to resurrection and transfiguration.

Chapter Thirteen

The day after, I went to work as usual but, before heading for the workbench, I knocked on the dusty glass panel of the office door and, without volunteering an explanation, handed in my resignation. As considerate as ever, Cyril said I did not have to give a month's notice, and that he would pay me for that month anyway. "And wipe that silly smile off your face" he muttered as he was filling in various forms for my benefit. "Did you find a better job? You are greatly appreciated around here, you know. Perhaps it's time we negotiated a rise?"

"No, Cyril. Many thanks. I'm happy, that's all." He looked at me intensely and started to smirk. "You... you are hiding something from me. I've got it! You are getting married." I burst out laughing, "Yes!"

"I'll miss you, you know." He hesitated then went on, almost timidly, "I will also miss the fitting sessions. You are by far the most beautiful woman I've ever seen."

"Why, Cyril! And I thought you only had eyes for the clothes."

"I pretended; I was lying. My eyes were lying. In a way, I wish I'd had the courage to tell you all this a bit sooner but, on the other hand, I am happily married, as they say. Even if you had gone along with it, it would have made life unbearable, both at home and here in the workshop. . . what with accusations of favoritism and God knows what else. No, it's a great pity, but it's better this way."

I was gobsmacked. I suddenly recalled a conversation with a friend of my mother's, a few years earlier. Her name was Antonia. She was an eccentric Scot who rolled her R's, always seemed to be in a good mood, had loads of gentlemen-friends, loved life and gobbled it up like a dog wolfing down its plate. The two women had known each other through a correspondence club when they were still at school. Mum never had enough money to travel up to Scotland. Antonia would then pop in from time to time and usually found an excuse to take us both to a good restaurant. She always teased me about the fact that I did not have a boyfriend. "Still a virgin?" she'd roar as she walked through the front door in a noisy fumble of holdalls, suitcases and umbrellas. I would turn as red as a poppy, but never resented her remarks. You simply could not hold a grudge against Antonia. There was something so genuine and so refreshing in that woman that she won you over immediately. One day, seeing that I felt a bit low, she took me aside, and said calmly and affectionately, "Stop worrying. You think your face is graceless, but have you ever seen what some supposedly sexy women look like? They are ugly. You are not. What makes them sexy is the fact that they truly enjoy sex. Men can feel it. Like most of us, you want a good sex life, but happiness doesn't just happen, my dear: you have to make it happen. And I'll tell you something else: when you do have a lover, other men will keep wondering what it is that you've got. . . what it is that makes him love you. Their curiosity will be aroused, and they'll start buzzing around like flies."

I have no idea what credit sociologists and psychologists would give to Antonia's theories. I most certainly never learned the art of making sex happen and I still don't know how to do that; nor did my affair with Peter stir a horde of potential lovers into action. Yet, with the announcement of my wedding, there was our Cyril, practically *declaring himself*, as they used to say in nineteenth century novels. The thought made me quite pensive. The lack of real love between Peter and me could have meant that I was not, at the time, wafting out that psychological - and maybe physical - pheromone that attracts men the way a she-cat in heat attracts her toms.

"And whom will you marry?" Cyril continued, "Not this Peter, I hope. I thought things were finished between the two of you."

"They are. And it's certainly not Peter."

"So, who's the lucky dog, then?"

"That," I said, pressing a kiss on his forehead, "is still a secret."

Chapter Fourteen

"You know," Lawrence whispered as if talking to himself, "there are people who don't like women's genitals. They like the beauty of women, their grace, their elegance, their vulnerability, but they don't like their genitals." We were in bed, satisfied, exhausted, yet still thirsting for each other. He was, almost absentmindedly, moving a finger between my outer and inner lips, brushing the clitoris then going down again. I was oozing but had, by now, ceased to marvel at this relatively recent development. From the very first time when Lawrence had made love to me, I'd had no problem in that area, and ever since he had asked me to marry him, I was almost continuously lubricating. "Are you talking about other women or homosexual men?" I asked.

"Not just those. Some women and most homosexuals find the intimate parts of a woman's body repulsive but there are many heterosexual men who don't like them either."

"Why are we having this conversation?"

"Because I am touching you and I am in awe of what I am touching. How is it possible not to appreciate such beauty? It's as if a man, describing himself as a gourmet, would declare that he doesn't like duck à l'orange or a twelve-year old Aloxe-Corton."

"Maybe his first duck was off."

And there we went: another bout of uncontrolled laughter followed by silly, recurring giggles. We had, it seemed, crossed a border and found ourselves in a new country, that of a god in three persons, *eroticism, love and mirth*, surrounded by *the landscape of eternal youth*. We shared our sexual fantasies and tried to turn them into reality. We were sinking into a warm ocean made of no longer impossible dreams.

Thus, it was that, the day before, we had gone shopping in a supermarket. I was wearing a simple, very short blue dress, a pair of sandals and absolutely nothing else. Very excited, Lawrence and I kept looking at each other and smiling. I could feel my heartbeat accelerating. I experienced the thrill of taking what seemed like an enormous risk such as leaning too far over freezer counters, stretching on tiptoes to reach a pot of jam on the highest shelf or crouching in the aisles for the lower displays. I could feel drops running along my thighs and almost wished that other customers would notice. Getting back to the car, we were laughing like a couple of idiots - wonderful, happy idiots with no allegiance to anyone but ourselves.

A few days earlier, Lawrence had called me at my mother's while I was packing a few things. In spite of my newfound happiness, I felt a bit scared. Serious changes in one's life always have that effect, don't they? I suppose that even a young Tatar girl chosen to share the life of a medieval Mongol Emperor in his palace, would not have left her smelly tent without a pang of regret. I wondered in particular if Mum would not feel rather lonely, even though she knew that I planned to visit quite often.

The phone rang. Lawrence said he just wanted to hear my voice. He repeated how much he loved me. After we'd hung up, I started sorting things out again and pulled towards me an old magazine that I could see sticking out from the top of a wardrobe in a chaotic assemblage of bonnets and scarves. As I opened it, I suddenly had to sit on the bed: I'd just had an orgasm - not a strong one but a very real one, all the same. For a long time, I remained motionless, delightfully groggy, unable to admit that it could have happened and wondering if other women had ever experienced such a jolt. At Cyril's, there was no shortage of "girl talk;" yet I had never heard anyone admitting to having an orgasm out of the blue. It was as if, through some magic link, Lawrence had sensed my momentary sadness. As if his ray of sunshine had pierced the gray layers of my fog. On that day, when I walked through the gates of his house – of our house – I could hear scherzos of happiness in my heart.

We both had to calm down, however, and face more down-to-earth considerations. Lawrence had two children from his first marriage: Louise, who had married a surgeon, and was herself mother of adorable twin daughters about to start senior school, and Urban, a computer brain box, the type of young man who can absorb technical knowledge as effortlessly as a vacuum cleaner. He had his own firm in Florida, something to do with CDs and DVDs. I had never met Lawrence's children.

"I'll have to get in touch with my solicitor and change my will," mumbled Lawrence.

"Won't your children resent losing part of their inheritance? That is, assuming I don't die before you do, of course. I may suffer from a brain hemorrhage in the next few minutes."

"Or a small meteorite could fall through the house at 100,000 miles per hour and pulverize you before my very eyes."

"What a mess! Imagine my body exploding like a tomato and spraying the whole room with blood and guts."

"The cleaning lady would have a fit!"

Typical! We'd be conducting a serious conversation but, thanks to this extraordinary attraction we felt for each other, an attraction we did not really understand, we would soon start drifting away. Lawrence made an effort to get back on course, "I can't see Louise and Urban having any objection. They are nice people, full of common sense. For years now, they've arranged for me to meet attractive widows, divorcees and even a few single women; always 'by accident,' of course. They don't need my money. Louise's husband, Ronald, is a consultant and a top surgeon. He probably rakes in something like £500,000 in a bad year. As for Urban, he is quite successful, thank you very much. You should see his house in Flor. . ." I interrupted, "Did you sleep with any of these attractive females?"

"Are you jealous?"

"Not in the least. Just curious. Like a cat."

"I've had two affairs. Those charming creatures were both called Natasha. Now, what are the chances? After all, it's not that common a name."

"Widowed? Divorced?"

"Divorced. I've already told you about them. Natasha number one was tall, daring, highly educated, refined. . . but her husband wooed her back. She fell for it, and they remarried. Can you believe it?"

"Is she happy now?"

"I doubt it, but it hardly makes me gloat."

"And the other one?"

"I've also mentioned the other one. She was wealthy, vivacious, charming but fickle and utterly selfish. A super girlfriend but marrying her would have meant jumping back in the furnace of Hell, and I'm not a masochist."

"So, you left her?"

"No. She fell for someone else, an estate agent who was trying to sell one of her houses."

"And is she happy?"

"No idea. I suppose the estate agent has had many successors by now, so. . . No, I don't believe she is happy. When you are a spoiled brat, you always want the other brats' toys."

Lawrence gathered the papers he had spread out over the glass-top table. He looked discouraged and sad. Oddly enough, I suddenly felt a bit low myself. The French doors were wide open. It was July but the weather had deteriorated. It wasn't warm. It wasn't cold. The sky was gray and depressing.

Chapter Fifteen

"Tell me, what sort of wedding would you like?" Lawrence was finishing a meal that I had prepared myself: chicken livers with risotto. He had been quite amazed when he realized that I could also be a good cook. We were on the patio where we ate as often as possible. A pale, sickly sunlight managed to seep through a wishy-washy layer of clouds. Lawrence never wanted a dessert. I got up to make some coffee. "I want a simple wedding," I replied. "Two witnesses at the Registry Office at six a.m."

"You'll have a job getting the Registry Office to open at six."

"You know what I mean."

I shivered as I poured some coffee beans in the grinder. Above all, I didn't want a wedding with pop music, a banquet in a hotel, a three-tier cake, bellowed songs, slurred speeches, lousy jokes and unsteady guests waving camcorders; but then, that is how things are done in <u>my</u> own little world and among those with whom <u>I</u> live. Maybe a wedding party in Lawrence's milieu would be quite different; held in the garden, for instance, with a marquee in case it rained, a top-notch caterer, soft music and priceless gowns. Maybe. . . Maybe. . . I didn't know. In fact, I knew so little of Lawrence! I suddenly felt very tired. It was as if I had to cross an incredibly long beach where I knew there could be treacherous quicksand waiting to swallow me. I desperately wanted to have a heart-to-heart conversation with Mum.

"It's called *fear of success* or *fear of winning*" Mother said, the minute I explained my discomfort. I stammered, "I . . . I didn't go after all this. I didn't spend my days and nights dreaming of Prince Charming. So, when he does ride in on his white stallion, I'm scared silly."

"Lawrence must have sensed it. He sounds as contrary as your father used to be."

"How is that?"

"When Michael and I started sleeping together, I told him I only wanted an affair: no marriage. Coming from a woman, this attitude was so unusual in those days, that it made him think. He came to the conclusion that a girl who was clever enough to reject marriage must be really special and that he should not let her go. Three weeks later, he proposed."

"And you said 'yes'."

"'Course I said 'yes.' That's what I wanted all along. Just relax, Jane. Lawrence knows you are not a gold digger, that's why he wants you. Otherwise, he would have said *see you in my dreams, darling*. By the way," she went on, "you are not the only one to be turned into an honest woman. Alma is also getting married."

"Alma? It rings a bell, but I can't remem. . . I've got it: she is the girl who caught a volley of buckshot in the face and is now blind. Who is the boy?"

"Would you believe Peter?"

"Wow! So, they made up?"

Mum got up to open the door of the mini-dishwasher (a much-appreciated present from Lawrence) as it had reached the end of its cycle. "Yes, those two have made up. The £600,000 she received from her personal insurance may have had something to do with it."

"Only now? Ten years later?"

"Alma's insurance tried every trick in the book to deny payment, then delayed the legal proceedings. Insurance companies should be called PLCs."

"Private Limited companies?"

"No: Perfectly Legal Crooks."

"And so," I added, "our dear Peter has gone back to his teenage love. What a coincidence!"

"Ain't it just? I happen to know that Alma's parents are devastated by all this."

"Who wouldn't be? However, if Alma really loves her lord and master - who knows? Maybe she enjoys being bossed around."

"They also say that Peter's father is being prosecuted for shoddy workmanship. If he is found guilty, that money could come in handy."

I took the pile of plates Mother was handing over to me and put them away in the wall cupboard. "Funny" I said, "to me, it's almost as if it all happened in the Middle Ages. I feel completely detached."

"Good for you. Think of your own wedding."

Chapter Sixteen

"How about going on a honeymoon?" Lawrence whispered in my ear as we were waking up, one morning.

"Are you making plans for after the wedding?"

"No. I want a honeymoon before the wedding."

"Really? And where would we go?"

"Anywhere at all. You decide. See it as a duel: I am the challenger; you have the choice of weapons."

I snuggled up to him. "You'll make fun of me if I tell you."

"Certainly not. Be extravagant. Be yourself. An Alaskan cruise? A Greek island? Angkor Wat? Go ahead. Even if you want to visit Graceland or South Fork, I shan't laugh, I promise."

"I don't want to go as far as that."

"Venice, Florence, Dubrovnik?"

"Mont-Dore."

"Where the Hell is that?"

"It's a town in the central highlands of France."

Lawrence propped himself on an elbow and looked at me. "OK. And what's Mont-Dore got that's so special?"

"The town itself? Not much. It's the surrounding countryside." Lawrence flopped back and placed his hands behind his neck. We remained silent for a long time. In the end, I couldn't stand it anymore, "Aren't you going to ask me how I got to know this part of France and why I want to go back?"

"I was waiting for you to blink first."

"You! You are the most horrible man I've ever loved." And I pounded his chest with my fists. His whole body was shaken with silent laughter.

I lay my head on this dear, dear chest and, stretching my arm under the bed sheet, started to play absentmindedly with a penis which, after the entertainment of the night, did not stand much of a chance to harden. "I'll tell you if I must." I went on. "When I was in what they now call "Year-10," my teachers got in touch with a charitable organization for deprived children. You know the type - those whose parents can't afford to send them on holiday. My mother and I had never done more than a day trip to the seaside. I was fourteen years old: the age limit for that particular scheme.

Everything was so new to me - the coach to Dover, the ferry, French trains that are so quiet, so fast! I was tall and very reserved. At first, everyone mistook me for a member of staff. It was a bit embarrassing. In fact, the staff were more interesting than the kids and I spent a lot of time with them. We ended up in a boarding school that must have been rented or turned over to us during the summer. Way back then, I promised myself that, one day, like McArthur, I would return. That's my chance. . . if it's alright with you, of course."

He just squeezed me against him. And another time, I thought I would tell him more about this wonderful school trip. About the two boys from a nearby summer camp, who managed to sneak into our dorms from time to time. They were never caught. It was all very lame, really. Someone would place a scratchy record of soft music on the elementary turntable and, with volume turned so low that it was barely audible, a few of us would dance with the boys for an hour or so, before we sent them away.

There were also nightly raids on one of us – we never knew which one in advance – by a small group of rather common girls who must have had lesbian tendencies as well. Every late afternoon, outside the dining-hall, they would choose a victim after a 'secret' meeting which looked like a rugby scrum. Later, in the dorm, shortly after lights out, they would rush towards the elected bed, remove blankets and the top sheet, take off their victim's nightgown or pajama and, when she was stark naked, someone would turn on the lights for a few seconds and all the other girls would go,

"Ooooooh!" Any one of us could have stopped that silly game with fighting and screaming, but resistance was mostly symbolic. I kept wondering how I would react if I was 'chosen' - but I never was. The whole time we were there, I remained really scared that it might happen to me, and at the same time, a little disappointed that it didn't. Obviously, my presence did not stir much interest.

There was also the day when, as we trekked through the mountains, and I walked behind all the others, I was suddenly overwhelmed by a moment of intense discouragement and unexplained sadness; so, I stopped near a brook and sat down, my back against a sloping rock, the warmth of which penetrated through my blouse. I could smell the fresh, watercress-like fragrance of the river. I closed my eyes, savoring the intense relief of no longer having to hear the chirping and yakking of the other girls, only the gurgling rush of water between small boulders. I was happy. I wanted this moment to last forever. A young Camp Counsellor, barely older than I, came back, out of breath, "Jane, are you hurt? Did you sprain an ankle?" I had no valid explanation; at least none she could understand. She yelled and screamed and told me off, using the same sentence over and over, but I wasn't punished. I understood, with hindsight, that she was supposed to be walking behind us; a rear guard, so to speak. She was more cross with herself than with me.

There was also a small donkey cart parked with its shafts in the air, and this stupid little brat who decided to climb into it just as I walked in front. The cart tipped over, and one of the shafts hit the top of my head. Pain and surprise mixed in equal proportions while I kept saying, "It's nothing, it's nothing. . ." I woke up in hospital and, indeed it was nothing: just the mother of all bumps. How can I consider this episode as being funny? It has always made me laugh, even during the painful few days that followed.

There were, finally, the disastrous picnics in the mountains: huge triangular, catering-size tins of the cheapest, most disgusting pork liver pâté one can possibly imagine. To quench our thirst, we were served some watery chocolate-flavored milk in dire need of chocolate and milk; for dessert, runny apple compote. Fortunately, the organizers sometimes came up with corned beef, which was quite acceptable, though served on half baguettes without a trace of butter, mayonnaise or salad of any description. It made my mouth so dry! If we were lucky, we were handed out oranges. Corned beef and oranges - the lingering taste of trekking expeditions during this summer camp.

And in spite of all this, or perhaps because of it (dreadful chow, horse flies and mosquitoes and no friends) I was itching to go back. Even at that young age, I had been impressed by the beauty of the countryside, but in the dark recesses of my mind, there may have been a less honorable motive: that of secret revenge. The feeling was a bit more subtle than revenge. It was also more noble than the showing off of a poor boy who made good, then returns to his village and parades in a Bentley. What I wanted to do was erase a bad experience and replace it with a better one.

I told Lawrence that I liked taking the ferry rather than the tunnel. I have nothing against the tunnel, which I see as a fabulous technical achievement, but I wanted to relive the conditions of my first trip abroad. "You can't go home," they say; at any rate I wasn't going home and, in fact, digging a little deeper within myself, I had to admit that I didn't want to recreate anything: on the contrary, I wanted to destroy something. I wanted to say - I wanted to shout, "Look, I am doing this trip all over again but, this time, I am traveling first class and with the man I love!" I was shouting this to myself. I was showing off in front of that awkward child I had been. I was stamping out the past and killing the child; I was starting to live.

*

Lawrence drove extremely well, without any hurry. I felt safe with him at the wheel. For the journey, I had plumbed for a dark red, almost black sweater and matching trousers. We stopped in Auxerre and ended up in a very nice, if rather nondescript hotel. It was called "Le Vieux Bouc." The food was excellent: not refined as in "nouvelle cuisine," but local, authentic and full of flavour. We went to bed early and just slept. Even when we didn't make love, there was nothing I liked better than waking up next to Lawrence, next to his living, breathing presence. The next day, as the weather was getting decidedly warmer, I chose a pair of shorts and a sleeveless, yellowish blouse with huge wooden buttons at the front.

The hotel Lawrence had booked for us near Mont-Dore left me speechless. Built entirely on one level, it was made of gigantic domes linked together by steel tubes. It looked like a collection of flying saucers that would have landed on a gently rolling landscape of impeccable lawns. Behind the glass-sided circumference of each dome, ran a deep-pile-carpeted circular corridor on which footsteps made no noise. The rooms, each the size of a two-bedroom apartment, started from that outer corridor and, becoming narrower, stretched towards an inner garden, also circular, of course, where Japanese-style blocks of granite on carefully raked gravel, kept company with full-grown poplar trees and abstract bronze sculptures. Ceilings were the highest I had seen outside churches and the whole place gave a marvelous impression of freedom.

I felt so elated that I rushed into the room and – something I hadn't done for years – I turned three cartwheels in front of a clearly astonished Lawrence. As I looked back, I saw him swallow hard and become quite serious. A haze of lust was spreading over his eyes. I knew him well enough to know what he was thinking and what he wanted. I undressed casually and, when naked, did the three cartwheels again for his benefit. He sat on the edge of one of the double beds. I sat on his knees, facing him, legs wide open, and threw my arms around his neck.

Sliding his hands along my hips, he whispered, "I feel sick to my stomach when I think that I might never have met you."

I kissed him. "And what about me? I feel exactly the same." We rolled over the bed and **christened** the room before we had even opened our suitcases. It was like the ritual of a couple of priests consecrating a new temple or, more prosaically, that of two wild animals marking their territory. When we recovered consciousness, the room had become temporarily, yet really ours.

Lawrence had talked about a honeymoon, and that is truly what it turned out to be. Perhaps we should modify traditions: honeymoons before weddings. The next day, we slept in, had breakfast and then spent the rest of the morning in the hotel's sauna and swimming pool. At lunchtime we had a very light meal. As usual, Lawrence and I ordered *à la carte*: just one main course; no first course, no cheese, no dessert. What a far cry from my summer camp food! I had the most delicate chicken sautéed in cream and white wine. Lawrence also had chicken but his was barbecued and served with a fiery, peppery sauce.

We decided to go for a walk. The footpath we chose went up the side of an extinct volcano and was wedged between thick bushes. We knew we would have to turn around fairly soon. Lawrence could walk much farther than one might suppose at first glance, but inevitably, his slight claudication meant that he couldn't go on for long. He was leaning on a solid, carved walking stick that, after sending postcards to his children, he had bought in the hotel lobby. I walked in front of him. The path was very narrow. I was wearing an adorable Jimmy Connors-style pair of white short shorts and a pale-green T-shirt. About one mile from the hotel, Lawrence grabbed my elbow and declared, as casually as if he'd been talking about the weather, "I'm dying to slide my hand up one leg of your shorts." We were crossing a thicket of small trees. The undergrowth smelt of moss, earth and nascent mushrooms. I pretended to be shocked, "Mister Drover, how indecent!" Then, giving him a hug, I whispered in his ear, "If you want. But why here? Are you planning to make love outdoors?"

"No. It goes back a long way, to the days of my very first girlfriend. She and I were no more than twelve years old. One late summer afternoon, as we had gone for a walk in the woods, she let me slide my hand up her shorts while I kissed her. I can't remember how or why it happened: it just did. I know I hadn't asked her. It came naturally to me, and she didn't object. What an extraordinary sensation! What a wonderful few seconds when my fingers went from one of her thighs to the other over the material of her panties! Sometimes, when I remember this moment, my heart still misses a beat."

I opened my legs a little. Lawrence's hand went up. He did not try to make me come, being content to move his fingers from side to side and brushing fleetingly the tops of my thighs. It was delightful. He had closed his eyes. I closed mine. When I opened them again, there was a very handsome old man looking at us: we were blocking his path. He sported a thin white beard on a long, suntanned face and looked very much like the experienced hiker with expensive boots and a well-fitted rucksack. Startled, I let out a little yelp and stepped back. Lawrence turned around and muttered, "Sorry!" The old rambler gave us a wonderful, wolfy sort of smile. "Sorry? I am the one who should feel sorry for interrupting." We let him walk past us. After a few steps, he looked back and added, "You are very lucky, both of you." Before we could reply, he had disappeared around the next corner of tall bushes.

On another occasion, Lawrence woke me up around 4 a.m. "Let's go watch the sunrise over the volcanoes."

"What?" I let him steer me into action like a little girl woken in the middle of the night and taken away in an emergency. He tenderly wiped my face with a cold flannel and made me drink a tumbler of orange juice. Somewhat less in a daze by then, I started getting dressed: a white man's shirt, tights (I felt that, in spite of the time of year it might be cold outside), light-gray trousers and matching cardigan. The night porter watched us leave with a turgid look through half-shut eyelids.

Lawrence must have done his homework, for he drove as unhesitatingly as if he'd lived in the area all his life. He wound his way up towards an impressive set of hills, almost mountains, dominating a campsite. He stopped the car on one of those lay-bys built for tourists who want to admire the view. We got out; we were, of course, the only ones there. The nocturnal silence seemed both warm and fresh, but also dry and damp all at the same time. A very light breeze was wafting in with a smell reminiscent of raindrops falling on dust; stars were shining fainter in the east. Our steps, on the platform, were echoing as they would have on a frozen surface. Lawrence and I leant on the semi-circular stone parapet built at the edge.

I was then able to observe the famous rose-fingered dawn of Homeric poems. Within a few seconds, the volcanoes on the horizon turned deep purple, the slanting light bringing out the lopsided rims of their – normally undetectable – gigantic craters. Purple became pink and crept down the slopes while crests veered to gold. I glanced to my left and whispered, "Look, Lawrence." From the valley that we dominated, and which was still in darkness, had emerged a tiny plateau touched by the first rays of the rising sun. It seemed to be floating on a black, invisible sea. Its vigorous green grass shone as if it had been lit from within and, here and there, appeared the white, grazing dots of a dozen sheep. I squeezed

Lawrence's arm as if I had been holding on to a life buoy. Faced with such intense beauty, I became scared. I had the painful impression of being within reach of understanding a great mystery - and yet incapable of doing so.

Chapter Seventeen

Yes, I had been dreaming of a simple wedding; if not at six o'clock in the morning, at least as early as possible, and only at the registry office. Alas, it seems that we can't always arrange these things the way we would like. When they got wind of my reason for leaving the workshop, my workmates uttered those shrill, ululating cries, now commonplace throughout the more illiterate half of the world's population. Even Cyril clapped loudly and shouted a few "wows" worthy of television cartoons for the mentally retarded. They asked me to draw a wedding list. I didn't know what it was. More hysterical laughter. Had I ordered a gown? No? "Excellent," they said. "We'll make you one. You'll see, it will be even nicer than Princess Diana's." *Shouldn't be a problem,* I thought, but bit my tongue.

My mother also said "Excellent," and added, "I never wanted to tell you, but now I can. I always dreamt of a real wedding for you, in a real church and with a real priest."

"I'm not sure you could call him a priest."

"A rabbi? Is Lawrence Jewish? Come to think of it, he does look a bit Jewish."

"He is not, Mum. Besides, I'd love him just the same."

"I should hope so. What is he then?"

"As British as can be. Well, not quite - one of his grandmothers was American."

"American? Come to think of it, he does look a bit American."

"Oh, Mum, stop it!"

We were, by then, giggling like a couple of schoolgirls. "Anyway," I went on, "That's probably why he is an Episcopalian."

"What on earth is that?"

I shrugged, "Not sure. A bit like C of E for the States, I think. All very respectable, anyway."

"Good. I was afraid it might be some kind of sect." She hugged me. "Everything is fine. I'm sure it will be a beautiful wedding."

I had never seen her so peaceful and so happy.

Lawrence and I went to see the Episcopalian minister. We took the train for London. Episcopalian churches are not a penny a dozen in Britain. Then on by taxi towards a green hillock in some leafy suburb or other. Nice vicarage; wonderful picture-postcard chapel: a white wooden building sitting on manicured lawn. The minister was a fat, jolly, instantly likable old man. "Look at that," he whined, as he showed us around the various buildings contiguous to the church. "Just look at that!" he insisted, pointing at a metallic-gray Jaguar. "I've spent my whole pastoral life in working-class neighborhoods. Now, look at all the luxury I have to put up with."

"Must be real tough," muttered Lawrence before I had time to sink my elbow in his ribs.

"Why did you change?" I asked, hoping that the minister hadn't heard Lawrence's remark.

"Health reasons. I was moved by my bishop. When my new parishioners saw me at the wheel of a battered old Ford Escort, they gasped and grumbled. They insisted on leasing this car for me. They didn't want to be ashamed of their pastor, as they put it."

*

Taking into account the ages of the bride and groom, that excellent man spared us the usual homily about *preparation for the responsibilities of married life*. We talked about this and that. Lawrence asked how much we owed for the ceremony.

"For the ceremony? Nothing; but you can bestow something to the church."

"It would seem," Lawrence answered with a smile, "that your church isn't in need of anything."

"True, true, but I will admit to a very human weakness: good, single Malt Whisky from the Isle of Islay. I wouldn't say no to that."

"For your church?"

"For its representative. The church and I are at one."

"No problem." Lawrence took out his personal organizer, "So, one case of Lagavulin and another one of Laphroaig for the Reverend."

"Good Lord! I was thinking of one bottle, not twenty-four."

"I insist. You can give the other twenty-three away if you want."

"Now, who'd be foolish enough to do that?"

It was obvious that the two men were getting on like a house on fire. The organist, on the other hand, wanted £200 per wedding, which seemed reasonable to me. We were introduced. His name was Robbie Lemanoir, an ephebe from California. Very formal and solicitous, he sauntered in, lips pouting, hips swinging lightly. Slim, and elegant, he was wearing expensive shoes, an open-neck cream shirt and matching trousers, all shouting, "designer labels."

"The drag queen is not exactly short of a bob or two," I couldn't help whispering in Lawrence's ear. Both of us could gauge the price and quality of garments at first glance. We started to smirk. The organist, realizing that **he** was the butt of the joke, glared back at us.

"Surely, we are not going to play the Wedding March?" he enunciated in a squeaky voice.

"Surely not!" Lawrence replied in mock outrage, his big eyes bulging in rightful indignation. He was trying to repress his laughter but simply could not. He burst out into silent, and then not so silent, laughter. I was in stitches and, to make things worse, the Pastor joined us. The situation had gotten out of control.

Our three shouts of "Sorry" came out at the same time. Standing in the middle of the delightfully comfortable living room with its beige leather seats, its deep-pile carpet and its wax-smelling New England furniture, Robbie had turned as red as a carrot. He was squeezing his legs together, squirming like a little girl who must go for a pee.

"Perhaps we could go for *The arrival of the Queen of Sheba?*" suggested Lawrence, anxious to extend an olive branch.

"Very well." Robbie turned around and left the room.

"I will choose a few hymns later and send the list for your approval. Any preference?" the Pastor added, while I was wiping tears off my eyes.

"I'm not sure. You decide." Lawrence offered.

"Excellent choice, Mr Drover!"

Chapter Eighteen

Dress rehearsal. Train journey. The week before, we had to pick a best man and a bridesmaid. After mulling over the problem, we plumbed for Lawrence's own children. Urban came back from Florida for the occasion. He was a cuddly, teddy-bear of a man who landed at Heathrow accompanied by his generously proportioned young wife. Lawrence's daughter, Louise, was very tall and distinguished with a long horse-like face, yet far from ugly. She had arrived the day before. At the rehearsal, she was quite splendid in a Mao-style, pink silk jacket buttoned up around the neck, and pale-blue trousers. Her husband, Ronan, seemed likable enough but displayed a very irritating, permanent half-smile on his round features.

"What is your specialty as a surgeon?" I asked, just to make conversation.

We were back at the Pastor's. It was raining and, through one of the windows, we could see, under a guttering pipe, a bright green plastic barrel overflowing with angry splashes of water orchestrated by powerful gurgles.

"Digestive tract," the surgeon answered. "It's a dirty job but someone's gotta do it." I could imagine him opening smokers' stomachs oozing with black stench or removing lengths of the large intestine.

Probed by the little devil in all of us, I asked, "And what do you dislike most about your job?" He answered without hesitation, almost as if he had been expecting the question, "Not being allowed to grow a beard." I could see in his eyes that he was really enjoying himself. "Hair, of any kind, forms an ideal jungle for bacteria." He went on, "I would not be against a law asking all surgeons to shave their scalps like Yul Brynner, or Telly Savalas."

I almost asked, "Do you like old American television series?" but in fact I had not the slightest desire to start a discussion on the subject.

I too was asked many probing questions. "The truth, the whole truth and nothing but the truth" Lawrence had made me promise during a sort of practice run, the day before; and he had continued, "Take heart, my children will undoubtedly be very surprised by your life story and, at first, feel somewhat sorry for me but they will not show it and, above all, will not belittle you.

They have never been arrogant, whether in private or in public, and I don't see why they should be starting now. Like myself, they form their opinions by the way people behave, and certainly not according to social or racial backgrounds; and when I say **behave**, I am not talking about the correct way of holding a fish fork either. I mean patience, understanding, generosity, absence of aggressiveness or vulgarity.

I think I did a pretty good job as a father, if I may say so myself. Louise and Urban know full well that their mother and I were at daggers drawn. They also know I love you. They will be very happy for me. It's a well-accepted notion that when we, wrinkly oldies, fall in love, it's for keeps."

*

My workmates had come up with a pale-blue wedding dress for me; so pale that it was almost white. To start with, I felt oddly disappointed by the choice of color. I realized then – and only then – that, down deep, I had always wished for a pink dress. I could not figure out why. Then, suddenly, and after all these years, the picture of an adorable teenager dressed in pink came back to me: a young girl whose orgasm I had witnessed, voyeur-like, in a dimly lit room full of jackets, raincoats and scarves, a young girl who had, afterwards, volunteered to help with the dishes in the kitchen. This fetish of my youth had always, in my mind, represented balance, quietly accepted happiness and the ability to be at peace with oneself.

Had I unconsciously been hoping that a pink wedding dress, like a symbol of my triumph over destiny, would grace me with a face as lovely as the one which had been haunting me all these years? Possibly. On the other hand, the color blue helped me sever all links between the new Jane and the old. The nightmares of my past had all too often been gliding in my skies like vultures touched by the last golden rays of sunset. The sky was clear now, pale blue with a hint of high-altitude cirrus clouds.

The cut and material of the dress were perfect, and soon won me over. It was made of satin; hard to imagine anything more attractive than pale-blue satin. I felt like biting it, rolling on top of it like a cat on a sunny patio. Tight-fitting from breasts to hips, it expanded, bell-shaped, down to calf length. A thin, almost invisible white veil was thrown around my shoulders and came down the front. I had specifically asked that there should be no train. The hat, neat and simple like a padded Asian bonnet, was in the same material as the dress.

The fitting sessions performed – I might almost say celebrated – after hours at the workshop, gave us all an opportunity to get to know each other even better. We laughed and joked like teenage girls; like teenagers, in fact, male and female, because Cyril was the only one with the keys to the building. He was not about to entrust those keys to a bunch of giggling young ladies. He had to stay – which he was more than happy to do – so that he could lock up. I would arrive at the fittings with soft-centered chocolates, or profiteroles and, of course, champagne. We usually came out with reddened cheeks and silly smiles on our faces.

This champagne and these decadent treats had inevitably compelled me to face the problem of money with Lawrence. Should I - could I - approach him and ask for money?

All of a sudden, I became as shy towards him as if I had reverted to being an obscure dressmaker having to deal with Mister Drover, a wealthy buyer who was showing up to inspect the premises. I decided to take the plunge, "I no longer have an income," I told him, shortly before the fitting sessions started, "and I would really like to take a few bottles of champagne to my friends. Do you realize that they didn't show a trace of jealousy or resentment when they learnt that I was going to marry you? I wish I could hug them all and then take them on a luxury cruise."

"Theoretically, that's not impossible but I don't see Cyril embracing the idea."

"I know, but I would still like to treat them to champagne."

We were in what I now call, *the house*. Lawrence, smiling from ear to ear, was looking at me. He had just unpacked a computer with all the latest specifications and was fighting his way through wires and foam wrapping.

Suddenly he became serious and said "Oh!" He had finally got what I was hinting at. He cleared his throat. He too seemed to have turned shy. "I see, I see," he muttered. Then he burst out laughing, "Another little problem we'll have to solve, I guess."

"How did you operate with your first wife?" I asked.

"When we were together, in a hotel or a restaurant, for instance, I always paid. I also took care of household bills, council tax, insurance policies, house repairs - you name it. Supermarket shopping? I can't remember. She must have used her credit card. She was highly regarded in her own field and earned good money - for a professor, that is. She taught entomology, you see. If she wanted a new dress, a pair of shoes or even a car, she paid for it herself."

I drifted towards the kitchen and started to make tea. Whenever Lawrence and I had to have a serious discussion, we conducted it around the small cast-iron table, and in front of a cup of tea.

"Got a bank account?" he asked, after we sat down.

"Yes. *Alliance & Leicester.*"

"Nothing wrong with that. How much did you earn towards the end?"

"Same as I did towards the beginning: the minimum wage."

Lawrence took a sip of his tea. "As soon as we are married, I shall ask my bank to make monthly deposits to your account. How about twice the minimum wage? It will be yours to do as you please and should keep you in knickers, as they say. For everything else, such as house bills, car repairs and the like, you won't have to worry about a thing. And talking about cars: can you drive?"

I was as red as the proverbial tomato and just nodded, "Yes."

"We'll have to find you a nice little runabout, like a Clio, when the time comes. Meanwhile, I want you to feel free to cope with your everyday expenses." He took out about three hundred Pounds from his wallet, "That should take care of the champagne."

I felt like shriveling to the size of a mouse and hiding somewhere. He reached across the table and took my hand, "I understand. I dislike talking about money."

I had met, usually by accident, people who were quite well-off but couldn't stop mentioning money, even small amounts, like the price of a toaster. Obviously, the rich are not all alike. Some, like Lawrence, have retained the ability to feel genuine empathy towards their fellow men and women. In other words, they are blessed with the gift of real class, something most wealthy people are quite certain they possess by the bucketful and by right of birth, while their arrogant attitude clearly shows that, in fact, they haven't got a clue.

My last fitting session was a little sad. I kept looking around our workshop. Casual visitors would have described it as untidy, messy even, with its iron railings running from workstation to workstation, pieces of material apparently just left on the benches for no obvious reason, baskets overflowing with swatches and samples - but that person would have been wrong: everything was laid out as it should in order to achieve the best results. One last time, I was able to inhale the powerful, mixed fragrances of fresh cotton and sewing-machine oil. *This bout of nostalgia is ridiculous,* I reflected. I had enjoyed my work but had never done it with the enthusiasm of a true calling or the sort of feeling that could have been generated by archaeology, violin playing, gymnastics competitions or even fashion modeling, for instance.

Old Goat — Donatien Moisdon

What I feared most – I realized rather dimly at the time – was that once I had money and belonged to a moneyed environment, I might run the risk of losing contact with reality. By necessity, we all live in a little world of our own. Radio DJs are convinced that listeners hang on to their every word; politicians that the whole country wonders what they are going to say next; train drivers that society's major concern is whether or not the 15:30 from Wolverhampton will have six or eight carriages. As for most manual workers, they take real pity on you if you cannot name a particular tool or practice of their trade. Yet, the world of the rich, in spite of first-class plane seats, horses, yachts, and second homes in the South of France – or possibly because of these things – remains the narrowest and most isolated of all. They have no neighbors, in the geographical as well as the Christian sense: only clones and rivals whom they always describe as "aaabslutly maaarvellss" while hating their guts.

Old Goat   Donatien Moisdon

As we got closer to the big day, Lawrence came to the dress rehearsal in a magnificent three-piece suit which must have cost him the yearly equivalent of my former salary. "I am rather disappointed in you." I whispered when we entered the church.

"Whatever for?"

"I expected to see you in that funny battle dress you had on, when you showed up at my mother's for the first time."

"Please, don't make me laugh or that poor organist will think we are making fun of him again."

He was there, of course, the poor organist, hidden behind the altar, sitting on the organ bench, his back to the chancel. I was feeling a bit guilty. He had done us no harm and I had no wish for him to become – even temporarily – the butt of our jokes. I walked over to him. When he heard my footsteps, he turned round, stood up and gave me a wary look, head slightly down, like a dog expecting to be whipped. It could have started me laughing again but I controlled myself. He had just finished playing a solo from one of Handel's organ concertos.

"It was superb," I said. You are a true virtuoso. What sort of organ is it?" I was sincere and I saw him relax.

"This organ? It's a Dunan. It was made in Villeurbanne, in France, near Lyon in the Rhône valley. . ." He was well away and on familiar territory. I learnt more about organs in the next fifteen minutes than I had in my whole life. I nodded and grunted my approval from time to time. He obviously started to think that I was one terrific lady. When I mentioned my genuine enthusiasm for Peter Hurford, I thought he was going to take me in his arms and hug me. He talked about the great organists he had admired in his youth: Power Biggs and Helmut Walcha among others. By the time I left him, we were best friends.

As I got back to Lawrence, I asked nonchalantly, "By the way, why did you show up at my mother's in that smelly overall of yours, the first time you visited?"

"I didn't want you two to think that I was. . .," he hesitated, "that I was courting you, as they say. You might have thought I was just a dirty old man."

"And you were not?"

"I'll take the Fifth Amendment on that one."

Chapter Nineteen

The big day arrived. Lawrence had hired a white Cadillac with chauffeur. In it went my mother, my two closest workmates and myself. The town hall is situated in a former big house perched on a hill overlooking what, in the 18th century, would have been a graceful park. Nowadays, among thorns and bushes, you can still find statues of nearly naked women, modestly draping a triangle of material over the interesting bits. After the formalities at the town hall, we still had to cope with a longish drive to the Episcopalian church on the outskirts of London.

To reach this rather unusual town hall, you have to drive up the hairpin of an unpaved road. It was cold; so much so that it almost felt as if it was about to snow. Soon we were in sight of the white fronts of the main building and its annex, both placed delicately on well-kept lawns where, here and there, grew elm and maple trees planted by long-gone landscape gardeners. I felt as if I had become an actress in one of these slow, nostalgic movies set in New England or the Deep South, movies which are not very popular in Britain. We prefer *action* movies if only, as Lawrence used to say, in order to enjoy a feeling of superiority over the Americans, whom we can then accuse of being an essentially violent nation.

We arrived early. The Deputy Mayor led us to the annex and to a large waiting room lined with benches. The seats were covered with a thin, hard layer of black leather. Lawrence's children and grandchildren arrived a few minutes later. There were a few slightly embarrassed greetings, everyone instinctively avoiding small talk. Louise's twin ten-year old daughters started running back and forth and were told off in whispers. Smells of terribly expensive but discreet perfumes blended with the scents of long-stemmed flowers placed in two large vases against the wall, at the front of the room.

I desperately wanted the whole thing to be over quickly. I felt limp and tired in the extreme. I would have liked to lie down on one of the benches and go to sleep, the way vagrants do in railway stations. I felt so out of place! Why had Lawrence insisted on a *real* wedding? Isn't that what women usually dream of? Well, count me out.

Immersed in my happiness, I had meekly gone along with anything he suggested. Yes, he had indeed asked me what sort of ceremony I wanted but obviously had also considered my answer as some sort of a joke. I should have told him that his wanting to marry me was all I ever wished for. He didn't actually have to go through with it. Still, within a few hours, or within a day at most, I would be going back to a normal life.

Going back? No: just going. What is a normal life for a woman who has never been married and has never enjoyed a decent standard of living? Should I get rid of the cleaning woman who came two hours a day, Monday to Friday? Should I do her chores instead? The work would not have bothered me, but I sensed that Lawrence would have disapproved. At any rate, I would have felt awful getting rid of someone who, like me, just eked a living from day to day.

Should I then join charitable organizations, visit the sick in hospitals and in old people's homes? Should I help collect clothing for the Salvation Army? I shut my eyes and propped my head back against the wall. What would my life be like now, I wondered, if my mother had not been so poor; if a reassuring absence of nerves had allowed me to pass my final exams at school; if I had gone to university or, if I had not been so plain-looking? What would have been my goal, my true calling? Would I have discovered what I was best at, and why I had been born?

"Can you look me in the eyes and tell me that you have really, actually written this poem yourself?"

"Yes, Sir. I did write it myself."

I could. . . I could write poems, short stories, novels even. However, if they ever got published, it would be under a pen name. Only Lawrence would know about it. It would be our secret. Suddenly, I couldn't wait - writing became, in a flash, what I had wanted to do all my life. Like so many would-be writers, I had unconsciously been afraid of other people's reactions, their scathing criticism, their sniggering. No one, not even myself, could imagine a writer who had never been to university. Yet examples abound, but like a prude who's afraid of sex, I had been looking for excuses in order to avoid admitting to myself what I really wanted to achieve.

I opened my eyes. Had I actually been asleep? As I removed my head from the wall, I felt a sharp pain in my throat. I placed my hands around my neck and moaned and coughed, then looked around me, feeling slightly ridiculous.

Not a sound in the room. Even the little girls, sensing that something was wrong, had stopped fussing and, wide-eyed, had sat on either side of their mother. Then some of the guests started shuffling their feet and others would utter deep, impatient sighs. I looked at the clock on the wall, Lawrence was late.

"Let's go over to the main building and to the room where we perform the marriage ceremonies," the Deputy Mayor suggested. "Mister Drover has obviously encountered last-minute difficulties."

Heads down, we traipsed slowly towards that room. The open space between the two buildings was drafty and viciously cold. I brought up the collar of an imaginary coat around my neck. We looked as if we were going to a funeral. In the foyer Louise spotted a public telephone and asked to be excused for a minute. "I am worried," she added. "We should have heard from him by now." But she got no answer. That meant he was no longer in the house. Still, she left a message on the answering machine, asking her father to call the town hall urgently.

We sat down in silence. Visions of a car accident, a fainting spell in the bathroom or a bad fall, followed by a broken hip, kept trailing through my mind. I suppose the others must have nurtured similar fears. Not for a second did I consider that Lawrence could have changed his mind or, following an attack of cold feet, had hopped in his car and gone away to hide somewhere in a Scottish wilderness. The Deputy Mayor was pacing back and forth.

Finally, he cleared his throat. "Ladies and gentlemen, you must understand that I have another wedding in a little less than half an hour. Let's hope that Mr. Drover was delayed by something trivial and that we can soon plan for another date. I am terribly sorry, but I must ask you to go home. . . all of you. Please keep me informed."

Stunned, disorientated, worried sick, we filed out of the town hall as, during a bad dream, evil spirits would fly out of a cloud. Louise phoned the house again, then the caterer in London. She promised to foot the bill. She then got in touch with the Pastor at the Episcopalian church and apologized profusely.

The Cadillac took us back. "But what happened?" My friend from work meowed constantly. At first, I would answer, "I really don't know, Michelle." She kept on with the same question, which became as hypnotic as a mantra. I stopped answering. Strangling her would have felt so good! I looked out of the window. It had started to rain. In the fields, now shiny with water, magpies were looking for worms. The Cadillac dropped my mother in front of her house and went on to "my" house.

When I got to the front garden, I was amazed to find that the gate, then the main door, were not locked. The dogs, soaking wet, did not greet me with their usual show of affection, only with high-pitched whining. They had obviously been left out in the rain, in the front yard. They rushed into the house with me and started to bark so aggressively that they almost scared me. They would throw themselves at the back door, stand on their rear legs and shake the windowpanes to the extent that they would have surely broken them if I had not intervened. The back door was not locked either. Once outside, Pyrrhus and Xenophon went through the patio like a couple of tanks, sending garden chairs flying out. It became obvious that Lawrence had never left the house.

My heart beating wildly, I followed the dogs on the central alleyway, between flower beds and bushes dripping with rain. My wedding dress had collapsed around me like the fur of a Persian cat fished out of a river. Around me, the dogs jumped and yelped.

And then I saw - the aluminum stepladder thrown to one side and Lawrence's rigid body rotating slowly under the biggest of the trees, his head grotesquely stretched, his neck elongated and bare. He was still wearing the beautiful suit he had tailor-made especially for the wedding. His black shoes were collecting water that had been running all over him. They had become gargoyles. I looked at his hands. His fingertips were dark. He had been dead for a while.

My head and chest on fire, I ran back and escaped towards the house. I was almost blind and suddenly barely able to perceive plants and garden furniture. I tripped a few times, fell headlong on the back steps and collapsed on a chair in front of the white cast-iron table.

Obviously, I had to do something, but what could it be? Should I try 999? I was paralyzed. On the table lay a small, hastily opened, padded envelope. An audio cassette had been taken out of it and bore a post-it sticker: For you "*darling.*" I shivered. I was both soaked and scared. I realized that instead of leaving a note or a letter of explanation, Lawrence had recorded his last message; but why put *darling* between inverted commas?

Breathing painfully, I inserted the cassette in the hi-fi stack. I had to have two or three tries as I was shaking so badly. I was expecting Lawrence's voice, and I yelled with fright when I heard my own voice, then my mother's. At first, I couldn't understand any of the words, so I rewound the tape, took a deep breath and started all over. I could tell from the light ticking sounds and subtle differences in background noises that I was listening to one of Peter's clever cut-and-paste jobs.

Me: Hi Mum, it's all arranged now!

Mum: So, that's it, then? Are you really prepared to marry your old Goat?

Me: Oh, yeah! He fell for it completely. In about a year's time, I shall divorce him and be entitled to one third of his money at least. Isn't that terrific?

Mum: Congratulations. Everything is going like clockwork. Good luck, dear!

Me: Right! Twelve months with the disgusting old bugger will be better than twelve months in the workshop, anyway. After that, I'll be free as a bird, and I'll have enough money to do absolutely nothing for the rest of my life.

Mum: Jane, you are the greatest. I am so proud of you!

I barely had the presence of mind and the willpower to take the cassette out of the stack. Should I destroy it, or should I send it to the Police? I painfully forced myself to think in a logical manner. If I said nothing,

Peter would obviously remain unpunished but if I made a fuss, my mother and I would be the ones being punished. With today's so-called justice, innocent people are blamed while the guilty will attract the unconditional sympathy of the establishment. And what about the stench of the tabloids? I would never be able to totally convince Lawrence's children that this tape was nothing but a nauseating pack of lies.

Better for them to speculate as to what might possibly have happened. Even if they came to the conclusion that their father suddenly could not face being married to a factory worker, it would be less painful for them in the long run. As for myself, what difference would it make? It would not bring him back. In a way, I too had lost my life and would not, under any circumstance, be able to win it back. I opted for destruction.

I hastily stuffed the cassette back in its envelope and shoved the whole thing in my miniature bridal handbag. It was pale blue and dotted with tiny golden flecks; then, and only then, did I call the Police. At that moment, I heard the familiar squeaks from the gates. Louise, Ronan, the twins, Urban and his girlfriend had arrived. . .

Epilogue

2002

In the course of a normal week, that is to say when school is in session, I start work at six o'clock. I stop at eight. I start again at four p.m., and I get back to my place around eight. When I arrive in the morning, I can hear the music of an opera coming out of one of the classrooms. We've got a teacher who hates taking work home; he insists on a clean and complete separation between his professional and private lives. He too arrives very early and stays as late as he can after the kids have left, that is to say until the caretaker kicks him out. Before and after school, he plays classical music. . . often operas, always very loud. I have borrowed CDs from him; I have lent him some. Like so many others, he wonders how it is that a school cleaner should like classical music, but I didn't tell him the story of my life.

Violetta's and Lucia's anguished prayers flutter amid crashes of buckets on the floor, squelching noises from mop ringers, or even the grating of stiff brushes against toilet rims. The singing gives up completely when competing with vacuum cleaners or floor polishers.

Appearing and disappearing like blurry ghosts, are short, banal sentences that filter in my mind through this whirlwind of sounds. Idiotic sentences. . . idiotic for anyone except me. . . sentences which, after all these years, simply won't go away.

"Your hands. . . so soft and warm!"

"And yours. . . so cool and smooth!"

I wipe a tear from my cheek. The other cleaners become solicitous, "Something wrong, Jane?"

"No. . . no. I am sorry. Just a temporary pain. It's over now. No, really, it's all over."

Made in United States
North Haven, CT
08 September 2024